The Horse that had Everything

WEEKLY READER
CHILDREN'S BOOK CLUB

WEEKLY READER CHILDREN'S BOOK CLUB

presents

The Horse that had Everything

By NEWLIN B. WILDES

Illustrated by Albert Micale

RAND McNALLY & COMPANY

CHICAGO • NEW YORK • SAN FRANCISCO

To HEATHERWOOD
—*a great horse*

DEFINITIONS

* (*asterisk before name of horse*) designates an imported Thoroughbred

Breastplate: three- or four-inch-wide piece of leather used across horse's chest to pull against in harness; or, with saddle, to keep saddle from slipping back

Bridle: leather headgear consisting of headstall, bit, reins, etc., by which horse is controlled in riding or driving

Close lead: to lead a horse with shank or lead line held close to the halter or bridle

Cuffing off: cleaning a horse

Dam: mare, mother of a foal

Fine: (as applied to horses): having clean lines of limb and body, as opposed to coarse lines

Get: the foals of a stallion

Girth: wide piece of leather or fabric that goes under horse's belly to hold saddle in place

Halter: leather (sometimes rope or other material) headpiece for tying or leading horse without bit

Hands: term used in measuring height of horses—one hand equals four inches

5

Lead shank: four- to five-foot piece of rope (preferably cotton) or leather strap snapped on to halter to lead or tie horse

Loose lead: to lead a horse from a relatively long shank, giving greater freedom, as in grazing

Off hind leg: right back leg

Pastern: the part of a horse's leg between the fetlock and top of the hoof

Pin-fired: small, deep punctures made by red hot iron, usually in- the tendons of the lower leg, supposed to cure lameness and strengthen the leg

Quarters: upper part of hind limbs

Racing plates: light shoes, usually aluminum, used on horses when racing

Snaffle bit: a single piece of tapered steel, usually jointed, used in horse's mouth to restrain or check it

Stud: an establishment for breeding horses

Tack: bridle, saddle, girth, or any equipment used on horse for riding

Tacking up: putting the tack on a horse

Thoroughbred: a breed of horse

Traces: very strong pieces of leather running from breastplate or collar to whippletree, for driving

Whippletree: pivoted bar on carriage or other horse-drawn vehicle to which traces are fastened

Withers: top of horse's shoulder

One

RICHARD JONATHAN (RICK) BALLOU WOKE AT SIX ON that particular April morning—not because he wanted to, but because something made him. The something was a giant tiger cat, Thomas Jefferson Tibbs, square-jawed, green-eyed, lithe, and powerful. T.J. had leaped easily through Rick's ground-floor window, had paused to inspect the room from the sill, and then, in another easy leap, had landed lightly on the bed. Now he was lying a foot from Rick's face, sheathing and unsheathing his razor claws, purring in deep-throated, pulsating contentment, switching his tail in spasmodic jerks.

Rick forced his blue eyes open, reached a hand out from under the blanket, and gently stroked the underside of the blunt, whiskered jaw. The purring rose to engine-like tempo, the sharp claws pierced the thin blanket, and reached flesh.

"Hey!" Rick said, coming awake, "cut that out. You hurt." The cat withdrew his claws. Rick lay there for the last precious minute, his blond hair close-cropped and almost white against the pillow.

Saturday, he thought. No school. Maybe something

7

good and exciting would happen today. You never could tell. The best things usually happened when you were busy doing something, when you least expected them. Maybe today he would get the call from Darwin Mears.

He got up, reaching for the faded blue levis on the chair, the gray jersey shirt, the blue pullover sweater. As he slipped his feet into scuffed loafers, T.J. jumped from the bed and marched dramatically to the bedroom door, tail hoisted straight up. T.J. did everything dramatically and with great poise. Except, very occasionally, when Albert, the tough Plymouth Rock rooster, disturbed his equilibrium.

Rick tried to keep the wide, yellow-waxed floor boards from creaking as he tiptoed into the living-dining room. Saturday was his father's morning to sleep late, in his room at the front of the house. On the long wall to the right of Rick's bedroom and across from the front door, was the portrait of Rick's mother that Kink Ballou had painted from memory thirteen years before, just after she died, when Rick had been just a little over a year old.

Rick always turned and said good morning to the portrait, because he felt that his mother was smiling at him and wishing him a good day. She was, he thought, a very beautiful person: her hair was dark and quite curly; her cheekbones were high; and, nicest of all, was the smile that was deep in her dark eyes and light just at the corners of her mouth. She would, Rick felt, have been a very wonderful person to know. She would have been fun and someone that he could have turned to for

"Hi," he whispered, as if she were really there

comfort. He loved her very much, though he had never known her.

"Hi," he whispered to her now, as if she were really there, and he grinned at her as he moved across the long room with its big pine dining table and captain's chairs at the far end. There was a giant fireplace of old and pinkish brick, a warming oven burrowing beside it, brass andirons gleaming. The rough-textured curtains were a cheerful red, the rugs worn, with deep, rich colors. In the kitchen, beyond, Rick put coffee in the percolator, turned it on, got a warm jacket, and followed Thomas Jefferson Tibb's stiffly erect tail out of the back door and into the first faint fingers of sunlight.

April—even late April—can be bleak and cold on a

back country Vermont hill farm. There were still spots of snow in the north slope woods, and, in the protected corners of the buildings, there were high, granular piles where it had slid from the metal roofs. It can snow in back country Vermont in May, even in June, but on this particular morning the sun had a touch of real warmth, and Rick felt that perhaps they would have an early spring.

He stood there at the back entry for a minute, looking out across the rolling hills to the north. Most of the time he loved Vermont for its solitude and its grandeur. Once in a while it was a little lonely there on the farm with only Kink. But not very often. The maples, the ash, the birch were stark and leafless now, across the hills, but the evergreens—the pine, and hemlock, and spruce—stood out dark and warm-green throughout the hills, and the fields lay quietly waiting for the summer warmth to bring them back to lush greenness. It was a big country, wonderful to walk and ride through, to explore. There were dark-bodied trout shadowy in the streams, the woods were full of deer, and, even on his and Kink's hundred acres, he had seen bobcat and black bear.

He yawned now, stretching. The chores had to be done, and it was also his morning to get breakfast. Suddenly there was a quick uproar, a spitting and squawking ahead of him, behind the shed, and T.J. Tibbs came out in quick retreat, ears tight back. After him came Albert, wings flapping, beak forward, moving in great, belligerent hops. The morning feud was on.

T. J. clung to a yard maple

Albert was a huge rooster, and his domain was the barnyard. His harem was small—only five gray-feathered hens—but he guarded them jealously, finding worms and food for them with a great to-do and clucking, calling them to him as they ran, looking like tightly corseted women running for a street car. Albert would not allow Thomas Jefferson Tibbs too close to them. No blood ever flowed, but the battle had been joined for years.

"You're a sissy," Rick said, laughing, as T.J. clung to a yard maple, tail lashing, ten feet off the ground. "Come on down and put the run on him." The red barn, white-trimmed, was a hundred yards away, beyond the post-and-rail fenced paddocks, the low sheds below, and, as

Rick walked out there, the small donkey, Abram, came around a corner and brayed lustily for his hay.

Rick and Kink had bought Abram one day when they had seen him tethered in a field with no shade, no water, and the sun beating down in hundred-degree heat. Abram had a nose like a pug dog's. Thomas Jefferson Tibbs slept on Abram's back on coolish mornings. The donkey had the run of the place, but he stayed quite close to the old mare, Rose of Washington Square.

"We do collect the darndest animals," Rick had said to Kink, "but they're fun, and they sure are personalities. They're company too, especially when you're alone a lot."

Rick gave Rose her hay in her box stall. She had a lovely head and a nice disposition, but she was heavy-bodied, sway-backed, and too old to ride. She belonged to a neighbor who had moved away and had never come back to claim her. That had been nine years ago, and Kink said, finally. "I guess we own her."

Maybe, Rick thought, for perhaps the hundredth time, as he fed the mare, maybe, someday I'll have a horse of my own, one that I can work with and make something of, and have as a real partner to explore the woods and back country. I'd like that, I think, more than anything. He was thinking of a horse like the Thoroughbreds that Slade Corcoran raised at Bellemead, five miles over the hills.

Rick threw some hay to Tenderloin, the white-faced steer, in his lot behind the barn. They had bought Tenderloin for beef and had fattened him with corn. "Boy, will he be good eating," Rick and Kink had said. That had been ten years ago, but they had never been able to butcher Tenderloin. He had grown a little fatter each year. "Heck," Rick said, when the subject came up, "he's a member of the family now." And, doubtless, he would be until he died of old age. Rick finished the chores and went back into the house. He was getting the toast and eggs ready when the kitchen door opened.

"Morning," a voice said sleepily. Rick grinned. "Hi," he said to his father. The man in the blue foulard dressing gown might, if you could foresee the future, be Rick, some twenty years from now, except that Rick would be heavier and taller. Kink Ballou had been a shortstop in college, quite famous in his league. He was on the small side, but quick and far-ranging as a player, with power in his good shoulders for the long throw, hands that were sure, and sinewy wrists that snapped the ball.

The hands were an artist's hands, long-fingered, strong, sensitive. Kink had turned to his real love—painting—as soon as he was out of college. There had been schools here and abroad, and now Kink Ballou was slowly moving up the long hill to recognition and success.

Portraits were his field, and there had been a show or two, arranged by his agent in New York, and commissions were beginning to come through. Not big, as yet, but growing. Kink was a quiet man, never making an issue of small things. "Upending peanuts," he would say about discussing trivialities. But on the major things he stood firm, unmoving. Living in Vermont, in the country, was one of those major things. His agent and some clients had tried to get him to the city.

"No," he said, his smile very pleasant, his eyes and jaw unyielding, "too many people down there talk about their work, but don't get much of it done." His studio was in the ell just off his bedroom, the big skylight making up the whole north roof. He sank into a chair now, running his fingers over the blond stubble on his cheeks.

"Why didn't you sleep some more?" Rick said, breaking eggs into a bowl.

"Couldn't," his father said. "Got to wondering if there was anything under that Morgan dame's makeup."

"Was there?" Rick queried.

Kink nodded. "I think so," he said. "Shrew. A lot of shrew behind that sweet smile."

"Going to paint it in?" Rick asked, a touch of anxiety in his voice.

Kink grinned. "Don't worry. It won't kill the sale. But I'll know it's there, and she'll know it's there. And neither of us will ever mention it."

He stretched luxuriously, yawning. Rick whirred the beater through the eggs. The telephone rang shatteringly. Kink didn't move. He never would touch the thing unless he had to. Rick picked it up.

"Yes," he said, "yes, Mr. Mears. She did? What do you know, Mr. Mears. Isn't that just swell. Everything OK?" A silence. "Yes, sure I'd like to come over, Mr. Mears. I can be there in, well, about two hours. Maybe less. And gee, thanks an awful lot for calling me, Mr.

Mears. Gee, I can't wait to —" The phone clicked dead in his hands.

"I take it," Kink said drily, "that was Mr. Mears."

Rick ignored the irony. "Say, what do you know, Pop," he said beaming, "what do you know!" His thoughts cluttered up his words. "That mare foaled about two o'clock this morning. You know, that good mare of Mr. Corcoran's. That Never Fear mare. The one with the beautiful disposition. The stake's winner. She was bred to *Mon Oncle. What do you know—she just foaled. That was Mr. Mears. You know, Mr. Corcoran's manager. He—he promised he'd call me. The mare is kind of a favorite of mine. She had a colt, too. Isn't that swell? I'd rather have a colt than a filly. Anytime. Wouldn't you, Kink?"

"Unquestionably," Kink said firmly, a glint of a smile in his eye. "Everything go well at the *accouchement?*"

"The what?" Rick demanded.

"The birth," Kink said, swallowing his coffee. "Mother and child doing well?" Rick's face suddenly went very serious.

"Gee, Kink," he said, "I guess so. Mr. Mears was, well, sort of funny about that. He just said I could come over when I asked him that. But I suppose it was OK, don't you? They don't ever have any trouble over there. They have everything."

"Yes," Kink said, "Slade never spares the expense. I'll say that for him. You going over right away?"

"If it's OK," Rick said, "if" . . . hopefully . . . "there's nothing you want me to do."

15

"Nothing," Kink said. "You taking Suzi?"

Rick frowned sheepishly, happily. "I guess so," he said. "I promised her I'd let her know. She'll want to go. She'll probably ride over on Ulysses S. Grant. I'm going on my bike. What do you know, Pop, a colt. I'd ten times rather have a colt than a filly, wouldn't you, Pop?"

"I think we covered that," Kink said. "How about the eggs?"

Rick spooned them from the pan. "I guess they got a little scorched, Kink," he said.

"I guess they did," Kink agreed, eating them amiably. "You won't be back for lunch, will you?"

"Gee, I don't know," Rick said doubtfully.

"You won't," Kink said, "and I'll clean up here. You're so excited you'd break all the crockery. Give Suzi my love."

TWO

I T WAS A MILE AND A HALF DOWN THE STEEP HILL AND along the flat by the brook, to the Bairds' farm. The road was soft from its first spring scraping, and rocks the size of baseballs made cycling hazardous. Rick was in a palpitating hurry, and he fell once before he came around the last curve in the narrow road. The Bairds' mongrel collie dog came running out of the yard and snapped at the leg of his levis.

The house was brown, with some of the paint peeling, and the trim was just a darker brown. A wide porch, that jutted from the front and sides, was full of a great billowing wash of sheets, faded shirts, overalls, winter underwear, and socks. Beyond the house was the towering, three-storied barn, with the sheds and milkroom to the west. The barn was painted red because red paint costs less than any other color.

There was a sign at the entrance to the driveway, a very handsome sign. Kink Ballou had done it. "Baird Farm—Purebred Jerseys" it said, in green letters on white. There was a handsome jersey cow as background for the lettering. Kink Ballou liked Tom and Lena

17

Baird and their daughter, Suzi, who now appeared around the corner of the horse shed, leading a horse.

"Darn it all, Suzi," Rick said, "I wish you'd teach Lady not to bite my pants leg every time I ride in here on my bike. Sometimes she nips through and it hurts."

Suzi ignored the request, as always. She was twelve, two years younger than Rick, straight and flat in a red cotton shirt, her tight levis tucked into high-heeled Western boots. Her face was round, with a pug nose, well freckled, and brown eyes that could be very merry. She wore her dark brown hair in two tight pigtails. When they had been younger, Rick had used the pigtails for swinging her hard about. But one day she had caught him square on the head with a rake handle. After that he had left the braids alone.

"Where you going with Ulysses S. Grant?" Rick demanded, indicating the horse—a chunky, short-necked Morgan, with a fine head, and a long, rough, matted winter coat. Suzi thought Ulysses S. Grant was the finest horse in the world.

"We just drove the cows down to the new pasture," Suzi said. "Pa finished fixing the fence. Nothing for them to eat there yet, but Pa thought it'd be good for them to get out a while. Where are you going in such a rush?"

The Bairds had eighty milkers—all fine, sleek, straight-backed Jerseys, plus all the young stock. It was really a four-man farm, but Tom and Lena Baird ran it with one hired man and Suzi. That meant long, back-breaking days and just a fair living.

Rick leaned on his bike. "Darwin Mears called me,"

he said importantly. "That good mare, Never Fear, just foaled, and he—he wants me to come right over."

"What does he want you for?" Suzi demanded.

Rick shuffled. "Well," he said, slightly deflated, "he promised he'd call me when she foaled, that's all. She had a colt. Do you want to come over with me?"

Suzi hesitated, desire in her eyes. "Gee, I'd like to," she said. "I'd like to see that colt. But I don't know. There's so much to get done. Pa says—" A fender-flapping pick-up truck swung up the rutted driveway.

"Suzi," the man said, getting out, "we've got all those sap buckets to get washed and stacked. Ma'll help you." He was a heavy-armed, thick-shouldered man in flannel shirt and rough gray trousers, with a wide, battered black hat on his head. He was handsome in a craggy, blue-jawed way, but the little lines of worry and weariness were already showing at the corners of his mouth and eyes. There are no hours on a dairy farm. There is only work to be done—at all times.

"Would it be all right if Suzi came over to Corcoran's place with me, Mr. Baird?" Rick said. "They've got a new colt over there. Just for a little while. We'd be back by noon."

"Sorry," Tom Baird said, "not today. Too much to get done. Maybe another time." He turned away, and Suzi moved off with Ulysses S. Grant. Rick stood there, feeling foolish and embarrassed.

"I'll stop by on the way home and help you with the buckets, Suzi," he said.

"OK," Suzi said, as she vanished into the horse barn.

It was four more miles to Bellemead, Slade Corcoran's farm, and, as Rick stood up on the pedals, forcing the bike laborously down the soft road, he felt guilty at leaving Suzi, and some of the fun and excitement had rubbed off of the day. But not all. And, when he finally came in sight of the great fields and pastures of The Bellemead Horse Farms, with their miles of white board fence, the excitement rose again, tingling, within him. He leaned his bike against the fence and went quietly into a low building.

The long foaling barn was warm and echoing quiet as Rick walked carefully down the wide aisle, dirt-packed, that ran in front of the dozen or so huge, iron-grilled box stalls. There were expectant mares in several of the stalls, and, down almost at the end, was a group of men, standing silently. Outside the stall two stable hands watched, big-eyed, their mouths open a little.

Darwin Mears stood in the open stall door. He was, people said, sixty-five if he was a day, short, a little stooped, thin-shouldered under a leather windbreaker that was always half zipped. His battered felt hat was turned down over a pair of startling, quick, keen, dark eyes.

Kink had told Rick, "Darwin Mears knows more about breeding, raising, and training Thoroughbreds than almost any man in the country. You'd never know it from talking with him, but you would by watching what he does."

Darwin Mears looked at Rick as if he did not see him at all. Slade Corcoran was in the box stall with Jim

Robbins, the veterinarian. As he came closer, Rick saw the beautifully fine gray mare, Never Fear, at the far side of the stall. As she raised her clean-boned head, the pain was still in her eyes. Then he heard Slade Corcoran say, "It looks to me as if the colt's off hind leg was twisted. Is it out of joint, or what? Did she have a hard time foaling? Did you have to do anything to help her?"

Slade Corcoran was over six feet tall, perhaps ten years older than Kink, red-faced, heavy-jowled. He smiled a great deal with his mouth, seldom with his eyes. There was a small roll of fat around the collar of the yellow turtle-necked sweater that showed above the smartly cut tweed jacket. He had on a cap of matching tweed, and tight-laced canvas leggings below perfectly flared fawn riding breeches. He was the country squire and he played the part. Rick never felt comfortable with Slade Corcoran. "His eyes," Rick had once told Kink, "are too small. Piggy." Those eyes were now fastened on Jim Robbins, the veterinarian.

Jim shrugged. "We helped a little," he said, "but it was an easy enough birth. There wasn't any force involved." Jim's face had that bland, innocent look which, Rick knew, meant he understood exactly what Corcoran was implying, and that he didn't like it—or Corcoran either.

Darwin Mears spoke quietly. "Nothing unusual happened to the colt in birth, Mr. Corcoran," he said, his voice low, firm as a rod. "The leg is off some, but it might be a weak muscle, or a pull, a pinched nerve. It could clear up in a day, a week, a month. Right, Jim?"

Robbins nodded noncommittally. "It could," he said. Slade Corcoran frowned. He was not happy. He was never happy unless he could blame someone besides himself for what went wrong.

"Well," he said, moving to the stall door, "we'll give it some time, but not too much. I can't afford to have a crippled colt around the farm. It looks bad for the stud and the whole operation. They're better off six feet underground." As he came into the runway he saw Rick.

"Hello, Ricky," he said, forcing a quick smile. "Bad news travels fast, I guess. How's your father?"

"He's well, sir," Rick said, unsmiling.

"Give him my best," Slade Corcoran said. He respected success, and could sense that it was coming to Kink Ballou. No one said a word, or moved, until he had walked the length of the runway and closed the end door. Rick watched Jim Robbins and Darwin Mears exchange a quick glance.

"Let's have another look," Darwin Mears said. He moved the gray mare gently to one side, so that they could see the colt in the corner.

All newborn foals are appealing. Rick loved them all, loved to be with them, to handle them, to watch them. There is something about them—bushy-tailed, wobble-legged, wide-eyed at the great new world around them—that catches at your heart. But, suddenly, there was something about this colt, trying to get back behind its mother, that was special, that brought a lump to his throat. He wondered what the future held for it, what masters, what pain, what pleasures. Would it be famous? Would it die soon? Would anyone care?

It was a big colt, larger than average, fine-headed, tall. But, as it moved, its off hind leg gave way, the hock swinging out wide, weakly, with little support, and there was a look almost of fear in the colt's eyes as it half dragged the leg behind it.

Rick forced himself to stand still and not move to it. Darwin Mears held the colt around the neck and withers. Jim Robbins moved the off leg gently. "What do you really think, Doc?" Darwin Mears asked.

Jim Robbins thought for a long minute. "I don't really know," he said. "There doesn't seem to be anything you can feel or hear at the joints—no bone grating. X-rays will help when we can get them. But, for a guess, I'd say the ligaments were pulled away from the joint, or they're completely undeveloped, or they just aren't there. It will take time, Dar, before we know for sure."

"If we get the time," Darwin Mears said shortly. He let the colt go, and they went out of the stall, slipping the bolt shut on the door. "I'll see what we can do about X-rays," Robbins said.

Darwin Mears nodded and walked slowly off toward the upper stables.

Rick wanted to follow him, to ask questions, to sympathize, but he didn't. He got on his bike and pedaled slowly toward home, thinking one thing—that he would be back the next day, and the next, to see the big colt with the worry in its eyes, and to do what he could.

"What do you really think, Doc?" Darwin Mears asked

Three

I T WAS AFTER ELEVEN WHEN RICK GOT BACK TO THE
Bairds' farm. Suzi and her mother, Lena, were scrubbing the great piles of galvanized maple sap buckets,
and then stacking them in the long shed. Rick leaned
his bike against one of the towering elm trees, and went
to work with hot water and scrubbing brush.

"How was the colt?" Suzi asked.

"Real handsome," he said, sloshing soapy water, "but
he's kind of—well, maybe crippled. Got a bad off hind
leg." He told them the whole story, what Doc Robbins
had said, and what Slade Corcoran had said about
keeping the colt.

"Is it in pain?" Lena Baird asked. She had black hair
pulled back in a tight bun. Her hair was stringy sometimes, because she worked hard and did not, as she said,
always have time to primp. Her hands were strong,
stubby-fingered, rough and red, but her face was wide
and bright, her dark eyes sparkling, her skin white and
fine, and, when she was dressed for church or a grange
party, Rick thought she was very pretty.

"Doesn't seem to be," Rick told her, "but I suppose
it's hard to tell yet."

"If it isn't in pain, Slade ought to give it all the time it needs. A year even. Trouble is," she said, as she submerged another bucket in the steaming water, "everything Slade Corcoran has has to be perfect. Right off and always. His cars, his clothes, and his house. He had a wife once and I guess she wasn't perfect so he divorced her." Tom Baird had come into the shed. He grinned.

"I thought she divorced him," he said.

"Wouldn't blame her if she had," Lena said.

"Wait a minute," Tom said, "Slade isn't so bad. Remember, he let us have that hundred acres of land at a fair price, and never pushed us about the payments."

"All right," Lena Baird said, "but he just doesn't have any feeling for animals. He buys his dogs because they're the popular breed that year. His horses are just cash registers at the tracks."

"A man can't afford to be silly about animals. Not on a farm," Tom said.

"Look who's talking," Lena scoffed, brushing damp strands of hair from her forehead. "You kept that dog, Fritzie, with her leg in a splint for six months, and hand-fed her, and lugged her everywhere in the car."

"Let's eat," Tom said, changing the subject. "Are you stayin', Rick?"

Rick stayed for lunch, as he often did, and helped all afternoon with the buckets. "Maybe you can come over and see the colt with me tomorrow," he said to Suzi, "if we get these finished." She nodded, wrinkling her nose as she gave him a quick grin.

Kink was in a dour mood when Rick, late that afternoon, pushed his bike wearily up the last grade to the white Cape Cod house with the green shutters. His father was sitting in a straight wooden chair tipped back against the house, smoking his pipe and looking down across the valley. His face was gloomy. Rick knew the signs.

"How did the painting go today?" he asked, bringing out another chair. Thomas Jefferson Tibbs appeared, purring loudly, and jumped into Rick's lap.

"Bad, very bad," Kink said. "I don't know why I bother painting these vacant-headed women. They ought to stick to photographers." Then he smiled ruefully, and added, "But they do make all this possible," waving toward the valley. He knocked out his pipe. "Like it or not, I have to go to New York and have a sitting or two with the Morgan dame to see if I can find something. Guess I'll drive down tomorrow." He glanced at Rick. "What's with you and Suzi and the foal?"

Rick told him. "Animals, animals," Kink said morosely, "the halt and the lame. They always seem to be with us." Abram, the donkey, peered around a corner of the house, joined the group delightedly, and pushed at Kink's hand with a wrinkled, importunate nose.

"All right, all right," Kink said. He got up, went into the kitchen and brought out some carrot slices. Abram consumed them noisily. Kink scratched the little donkey's ears. "I suppose," he said, "that you'll be up at Corcoran's quite a bit from here on."

Rick hesitated. "I just want to see what happens to that colt," he said. "He's so handsome and he looks so frightened, and sort of worried. But I'll keep things in shape here while you're away."

Kink got up. "I know you will," he said. "But right now, how about doing up the chores while I get the fire going for the steak?"

As Rick fed the animals at the barn, his thoughts kept going back to the colt, wondering whether, as Lena had asked, it was in pain.

Early the next afternoon Rick picked Suzi up on his way to Bellemead and the foal. Suzi was bareback on Ulysses S. Grant when Rick pedaled his bicycle into the Bairds' yard. The little Morgan was so fat and chunky that Suzi's legs stuck out almost straight from his sides.

"Are you going to take that bike, or do you want to ride double on Ulysses?" Suzi asked, as the horse moved around, eager to be off.

"I'll stay on the bike," Rick said. "He bounces and jars too much when he trots, and he keeps putting in those little bucks."

"He just feels good," Suzi said. "It's spring. Didn't you know? Do you want to use the hitch?"

The hitch was something that they had developed for long trips, or just for fun. Rick went into the barn and brought out the breastplate, traces, and the light whippletree from an old buggy. To the whippletree they had attached a quarter-inch rope, which ran back some fifteen feet and fastened, with a special pull knot that could be loosened quickly, to the front bar of Rick's bicycle. When Ulysses S. Grant trotted or cantered, Rick had nothing to do but sit on the bike and steer. But

*The hitch was something they had developed for long trips—
or just for fun*

when the horse walked, Rick had to pedal enough to
keep the bike stable.

The hook-up caused some comment around the
countryside, but it had expanded their travel area by
several miles. The first time they had used it, Ulysses S.
Grant had been quite perturbed by the strange con-
traption dragging behind him. He had run almost a
quarter of a mile before Suzi had quieted him, and then
he kept turning his head and watching the bike until he
decided that everything was all right. Now he appeared
to like the arrangement.

"OK," Rick said from his bike. Ulysses S. Grant took

up the slack slowly, then trotted off, pulling his passenger, ears flicking delightedly.

Doc Robbins' car was at the foaling barn when they came up. They tied Ulysses S. Grant and went silently into the barn.

Down at the gray mare's stall Darwin Mears and Jim Robbins were just carrying out what Rick recognized as the portable X-ray machine. He and Suzi peered through the bars of the stall. The colt was stretched out flat on its side, breathing deeply, gustily. The mare nuzzled it.

"Is—is he OK?" Rick blurted, eyes big.

"He's all right," Darwin Mears said. "We had to give him a sedative so that Jim could get the pictures. He'll be back on his feet quick enough."

Doc Robbins picked up his bag and moved off. "I'll get these developed and give you a call," he said.

Darwin Mears pushed his old felt hat high on his forehead, and watched the gray mare. Maybe, Rick thought hopefully, this will be one of the times when he will talk.

"You never know," Mears said, half to himself. "This figures to be, from breeding and bloodlines, as good a foal as I've ever seen. And he appears to be, too. He's a big, good-bodied, good-headed youngster. And then this. You never know."

"What," Rick almost whispered, after a long silence, "do you think is the matter with him?"

The manager rubbed a stubbly chin. "The best guess now," he said, "if it isn't a joint injury, if the X-rays don't show anything, is that it's either a nerve injury that affects the muscles, or even a muscle tear. Probably the first."

"Can it be cured, or fixed?" Suzi asked. "What do you do, Mr. Mears?"

Darwin Mears shrugged. "Time," he said, "time and sun and work, and this and that you can do. But mostly time."

The foal was beginning to move its long legs. "Is it all right," Rick said almost pleadingly, "if I come and see him? Pretty often? Every day, maybe?"

Darwin Mears turned and looked at the young, very eager, handsome boy, and at the big-eyed girl with him. Then he smiled. "You like them, don't you," he said. "Some people really like them. And that's reward enough. Sure, come and see him as much as you like. Good for him, good for you too, both of you. How's your father, Suzi?"

"He's fine, Mr. Mears," Suzi said.

"Good farmer. One of the few left," Darwin Mears said. He turned back to Rick. "I've got a three-year-old I'd like to see move around the track," he said. "Do you want to work him for me? Just slow."

"Gee," Rick said, the thrill choking him, "gee, I sure do, Mr. Mears. You bet." In the last year or so Darwin Mears had let him work several young horses on the training track. Those had been big days, red-letter days.

"Come on," the gray-haired man said, and they moved on up to the big stables. "Do you know," Darwin Mears said abruptly, "why I let you on these young horses?"

"No, sir," Rick said.

"Because of your hands," Darwin Mears said. "Gentle. Firm. Like springs. Most important thing a horseman can have. If you have good hands you usually have the other important things—patience, feeling. Some people are born with 'em."

They all went into the big tackroom that housed the bridles, girths, and exercise saddles soaped to a dull rich gleam, the bits and hardware bright, row on row.

"Put some tack on Times Three, will you Jimmy," Mears called to a stableman, "I want to watch him move."

It was a wonderful afternoon for Rick, light on the bay Thoroughbred, the wind quick in his face, the thrill of the slow canter, the fast burst, the young horse moving with floating grace, ease, and power.

"Gee," Suzi said, as they started home, "are you ever lucky. I wish I could ride one of those."

"When you're older, maybe," Rick said condescendingly, head still in the clouds. Suzi put her cheek against Ulysses S. Grant's rough, matted neck and patted him quickly.

"Are you really coming over to see that colt every day, Rick?" she asked.

He nodded. "I wonder what those X-rays will show," he said.

Early the following week he found out.

Four

O N TUESDAY MORNING RICK SAID TO MRS. AMYOTT, who lived down the road a piece, cleaned for the Ballous, and stayed in the house when Kink was away, "I may be a little late for dinner. I'm going over to Corcoran's after school, to see a colt."

That day, instead of taking the local bus, which ordinarily picked him up at the foot of his hill, he rode his bike the two miles to the small country school. He was in the last grade there, the eighth. Next year he would take the long bus ride to Woodville Union High, nine miles away. He looked forward to that, except that Suzi wouldn't be going for two more years.

It was almost four o'clock when he pedaled up to the foaling barn. Inside, Slade Corcoran, Doc Robbins, and Darwin Mears were at the stall. "All right," Slade Corcoran was saying, "so the X-rays show no bone damage. So you say it's a pinched nerve, affecting a muscle, or a muscle tear. How long before we really know what we do have? If we have anything."

Jim Robbins shook his head, that bland look, concealing dislike, on his face. "Hard to say, really," he said. "A year. Maybe quite a bit less."

Slade Corcoran grimaced. "As usual," he said unpleasantly, "you doctors won't commit yourselves. Maybe that. It's possible that—and on the other hand. Well, I'll commit myself. I'll say that if this colt isn't square and sound in ninety days—out! He goes down. My business is sound stock. A cripple can ruin a stallion's value overnight. And *Mon Oncle is too valuable a property. Ninety days." He turned to leave and saw Rick.

"Hello, Ricky," he said, trying to bring pleasantness back into his face and voice. "I saw you working a three-year-old Sunday. Those are the ones to spend your time on. Not the cripples. My best to your father." He walked away, the jacket tight across his thick shoulders, the bunch of feathers gay on his Tyrolean hat.

Jim Robbins shrugged and left. Rick and Darwin Mears stood gazing at the mare in the clean, knee-deep straw. After a minute a tiny, concave forehead peered around the mare's shoulder, and the foal watched them. "Sometimes," Darwin Mears said, "it scarcely seems worth it—even at the money he pays."

The foal came around and began nuzzling its dam for milk. It was so big for its age, so alert, so perfect, except for that dragging leg.

"Does the leg hurt it?" Rick asked.

Darwin Mears shook his head. "Seems not," he said. "Doc tested it pretty carefully."

"Is there anything I can do to help?" Rick said. "I— I'll probably be over here most every day."

The Bellemead manager looked at him, and then

looked away. "Well," he said, "you can start handlin'
the little guy. Right now. Run your hands over him. Tap
his feet. Get his confidence. Then, maybe in a week or
so, when he knows you, you can start pickin' up his feet,
and you can massage that leg. I'll show you how. Mostly
it's time. Which we don't seem to have much of."

"When can I give him carrot bits?" Rick asked.

"Ten days or so. And not too many."

"I just want it so he'll look forward to seeing me,"
Rick said, and Darwin Mears nodded.

"Do you think he'll be gray, like his dam, Mr. Mears?"
Rick wanted to know.

"We'll know in six months or so, when he sheds his
baby coat," the old man said, "providing—" He left the
sentence unfinished.

It was after six o'clock and very dark when Rick
rode the bicycle into his dooryard. He did up his chores
and was glad that Mrs. Amyott was there to have dinner
ready.

For the next ninety days he saw the colt almost
every day.

May had brought some warm days, and the foal was
often out with its dam—not in the big pastures with the
other mares and youngsters, but in a small one near the
barn, so that it would not be hurt by the other animals,
or strain itself too much. It began, as the days passed, to
recognize Rick's voice, and to peer at him from its dam's
side. Once in a while it would come to him, tentatively,
and stand with him for a minute or so, before scurrying

back to maternal safety. But it was in the stall, as darkness fell and the animals were brought inside, that Rick did his work.

There the colt began to accept him, to stand as, at first, he merely tapped the tiny hoofs. Then he tried picking up a foot, and that took days. But carrots are enticing and, in a month or so, the little fellow held up his foot voluntarily, then turned his head for the reward.

Darwin Mears showed Rick how to massage the ailing leg. "Just rub it easy, but strong enough to get the blood movin', to strengthen the muscle."

The muscle, or the nerve, or whatever the trouble was, did not seem much better. The leg dragged, and it tore Rick's heart to see the little fellow try to cavort and play, with the leg so helplessly weak.

Kink came over one Sunday. Slade Corcoran happened to be at the barns and talked with him.

"I can see his point," Kink said at home that evening. "A crippled animal—especially a horse that will be big and hard to care for—just can't be kept around. Especially around a stud farm, with buyers coming and going."

"But Jim Robbins said maybe a year," Rick protested, "and Mr. Corcoran won't give it that much time." Kink shrugged.

"I'm getting more worried about you, fellow," he said. "You've been pushing that bike ten miles almost every day. You've lost some weight. We can't have you getting sick."

"I'm all right," Rick said. "My marks are up at school,

and I get my chores done. Besides, he—he needs me. He's beginning to count on me. He whinnies now, when he sees me. The funniest, shrill little whinny. And he comes to me."

Kink looked at the boy's face, and the expression as he talked about the colt. "All right, son," he said quietly, "all right."

Suzi was much more encouraging. "I think he's better," she said in mid-June. "I don't see him every day, the way you do, and I can notice a difference. Maybe the massage is doing it. Or," she added with that imp of a grin, "the carrots."

The colt had its own feed box now, and was eating crushed oats with its mother.

"I really think he is going to be gray, Mr. Mears," Rick said one evening, when the two were watching the youngster in its stall.

"Could be," Mears admitted. "He'll be almost black at first, then steel gray. He sure seems to take to you."

"I can put his halter on and loose lead him now," Rick said proudly. "I bet in another week or two I can close lead him, right at the halter, and keep him steady beside me."

Mears looked at the boy's thin face, the bright blue eyes peering at the colt. There was something in those eyes that made him turn away quickly, made his voice a little gruff. "Likely he'll do anything you ask him to before long," he said.

School was over and they were halfway through

July when the big afternoon came, the afternoon that capped it all, that make-or-break afternoon.

It was hot and humid that day. Rick was sitting under a great maple in the paddock with the mare, Never Fear, and the unnamed colt. He had massaged the colt until the youngster had become fed up with the handling and had swung away, ears back. Then he had turned and come back to Rick, ears forward, making amends, looking for the inevitable carrot slice.

Slade Corcoran walked down over the lawns and through the trees from the big brick mansion on the rise. He had on lightweight jodhpurs and a salt sack riding coat. A bamboo crop was swinging from one hand. He had seen Rick there with the mare and colt many times during those past three months, sometimes as he drove by in his Jaguar, sometimes as he rode one of the solid, quiet hunters.

"Ricky," he had said once, "I appreciate what you're doing. Darwin has told me. But I'm afraid you're wasting your time. You should be working the two-year-olds."

Rick had said, "But you don't mind, do you, sir?"

Slade Corcoran had shrugged. "No, I don't mind, it's up to you." Darwin Mears joined him now and, as they came up to the paddock, Doc Robbins' jeep pulled into the yard.

"I want to see him move around, really move," Corcoran said. The heat always made him unpleasant. "You'd better get out of the paddock, Rick," he ordered.

Darwin Mears went in and made the colt move out briskly. The leg swung out at the hock, letting the off hip down. The canter was not a hobble, but it was uneven, dragging.

"I don't see that he's any better," Corcoran said. "Appreciably, that is. What do you say, Doc?"

"He's some better, I think," Jim Robbins said cautiously. "Seems like a straighter action."

"Look," Slade Corcoran said, "let's not have a lot of wishful thinking. Let's be realistic. *I* will be, anyway. I say this colt's a cripple, probably always will be a cripple—as far as being useful to me is concerned. And I say, put him down."

"No!" Rick said it involuntarily, his voice loud, startling. The three men looked at him. Slade Corcoran checked what he was going to say, remembering Rick's father, remembering success.

"Don't put him down, Mr. Corcoran," Rick said, his

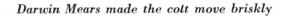

Darwin Mears made the colt move briskly

voice going husky, then shrill, "I've worked with him and I know he's going to get better. If you don't want him, I do. He—he counts on me. He really does."

Slade Corcoran frowned. "What would you do with him, Ricky? He's a crippled colt."

"I don't know, sir," Rick said, "not yet, anyway. All I know is that I want him, and he needs me. And, gee, I guess I need him too, Mr. Corcoran."

The silence was long. The colt stood in its dam's lee, watching.

"The boy has bicycled over here, ten miles, almost every day," Darwin Mears said quietly.

Slade Corcoran considered things, his lips pursed tightly, eyes narrowed. "Can the colt be taken from the mare right away?" he asked.

"In a few days we can dry her off enough," his manager said.

Slade Corcoran turned to Rick. "I don't know why I'm doing this," he said, "except that I like your father, and I like your determination. You can"—he chose his words carefully—"have this colt. *Provided*. Provided you get him out of here within—within a week. Provided you keep him out of my sight. And provided that you never volunteer anything about his breeding, or that he came from Bellemead. Do you understand?"

"Yes, sir," Rick said. Slade Corcoran turned and walked away, up through the trees, and Rick, suddenly, began to cry. It made him very angry to cry, and he tried to stop the tears that were coming down his cheeks, but he was very tired and he couldn't stop. Darwin Mears and Jim Robbins went into the barn, and, after a minute or two, the boy's shoulders stopped shaking. Darwin Mears came out alone a while later.

"We'll fix things up and get him over to you in the trailer," he said. "That won't be any problem, boy." He put his hand quickly on the boy's shoulder and then went up the drive. After a while Rick got his bicycle and started home. He had to see Suzi now. And his father. His father would have to let him take the colt. He would simply have to.

Suzi glowed. "Oh, Rick," she said, standing behind one of the big double-unit milking machines in the hot, low-ceilinged cowbarn, as he told her, "that's wonderful, simply wonderful. And I know, I just know that he'll get better."

Tom Baird wasn't so optimistic. "You've bit off something, boy," he said doubtfully. "Spend an awful lot of time and then maybe have nothin' to show for it except grief."

But Lena Baird encouraged him. "Maybe it is a gamble, Rick," she said, putting down one of the heavy milk pails, brushing the dark hair back from her eyes, "but it's the kind of thing you have to do to make life worth living, to give it a little hope, and purpose and excitement. Some day you'll know what I mean. I'm glad you're taking him. And we'll help, too."

She paused, thinking, and then her face brightened with interest and she said, "Skimmed milk, Rick, that's

"Skimmed milk, Rick, that's the thing to give him," Lena said

the thing to give him. With a little lime water in it. Does wonders. My father used it with foals. And we have plenty of skimmed milk, don't we, Tom?"

Tom Baird nodded. "Guess so," he said, "but I'll tell you one thing, Rick. You want to have a good, high-boarded stall to put that colt in for the first few days. They can raise Cain when they're first taken from the dam. And don't have any loose buckets or grain boxes or things he might hurt himself on, bouncing around. I've seen 'em go right up the side of a wall, trying to get back to their mother."

Kink was working in his garden when Rick pushed the bicycle up to the house late that afternoon. He told Kink the story, words tumbling fast over each other, while his father was still on his knees in the flower garden. When he was through, and waiting, almost holding his breath, he had one last word. "He needs me, Kink. And I guess I need him, too."

Kink got up slowly, and walked to one of the lawn chairs. He sat down, and looked at the boy, not saying anything for what seemed minutes—just looking, thinking.

And, as he sat there with Rick in front of him, the big cat, Thomas Jefferson Tibbs, came quietly up on velvet paws, purring against Rick's leg. Then a pug-nosed muzzle peered around the corner of the house as Abram came to join them. In the distance, from the barn, came the deep bellow of Tenderloin demanding his evening grain, and, in between, the excited voice of Albert, the rooster, summoned his harem to a worm or two. It happened all together and suddenly Kink grinned, and the grin showed the love he had for his son, the understanding he had of him.

"Sure, Rick," he said, "sure. I think it's a fine thing. Everyone wants to be needed. It's important to us all." Rick felt the tears well up behind his eyes. He was determined not to cry again, and he didn't. And, if his father had asked him then to do anything, anything in the world, he would have tried to do it. No matter what.

"I guess," he said, after a while, "that we'd better have a pretty strong stall for him. For the first few days anyway." He told Kink what Tom Baird had advised, and his father nodded.

"We can fix one up, you and I, in the corner of the

43

barn. We've got plank enough. Let's go have a look."
They walked out to the barn. On the way Thomas
Jefferson Tibbs got a quick clawful of feathers as he
crept up behind Albert, who was too busy finding food
for his hens to protect his rear.

The red barn was not large—some forty feet long
and thirty wide—with big doors at each end. On the
left were two box stalls, each opening to a separate
paddock, where the old mare, Rose, and Tenderloin
could graze out in adjoining post-and-rail fenced paddocks that stretched a hundred yards into the meadows. The floor was dirt, packed almost cement-hard
over the years. The supporting posts made an ideal
place for another box stall, perhaps twelve feet square,
adjoining Tenderloin's.

"This looks all right," Kink said.

"Sure," Rick agreed, "and we can cut another door
so's he can run out beside the others."

"Which means another row of post-and-rail fence,"
Kink said. "We'll get at the stall tomorrow."

Five

As RICK TRIED TO GET TO SLEEP LATE THAT NIGHT IN his ground-floor bedroom, the thought kept coming back, "I own him now. He's mine, and it's all up to me what happens to him."

Four days later Darwin Mears brought the horse trailer into the yard.

"Lucky thing you got him to lead," Mears said, climbing stiffly out of the truck cab, "else we never maybe would have got him loaded." He went to the back of the trailer, and Rick peered over the high tailgate with him. They had removed the stall partition, so that there was room for the colt and the two stablemen who were holding him.

"Ride all right?" Mears asked.

The men grinned. "He's sure strong," one said. "Took all we had to keep him on the floor."

The colt's eyes were big, terrified, red-rimmed. The whinny came almost as a scream, shaking the whole small, woolly body, as the youngster demanded its mother. Mears dropped the tailgate. The men led the colt out. The off hind leg dragged, but strength pulsated from every other part of the small animal. His brush of a tail wagged. He bounced against the restraining lead shanks. Rick spoke to him, trying to quiet him, but the colt did not, apparently, recognize him.

He was going to be gray, Rick thought, no question about it.

"Let me have a shank," he said, and talked quietly again to the little fellow, his hand on the small withers.

"Lead him around a bit," Darwin Mears said. "Let him have a look at things."

The colt would take a bite of the thick grass, and then seem to ignore the mouthful as the frantic whinny shook its body again.

"You may have to coax him some to get him to eat and drink. Can you get skimmed milk for him?"

Rick said he could.

"Fine," Mears went on. "I've got it all written down here, how much and what he should get for a while. After that you'll know, or you can ask." He gave Rick the folded paper. Then he moved to one side, motioning Rick with him.

"I hope," he said, his face deep-furrowed and serious, his eyes a glint of brown, "that this works out for you, boy. Anything I can do, you ask me. But"—and he peered intently at the boy—"there's one thing I do want to tell you." He paused. "People will say," he continued, "that you never should make a pet of a colt. And," with a slight, quick nod, "I'll agree with 'em. Provided you say what a pet is. A pet, to me, is a lap dog, or something that people kowtow to. An animal that runs the show. A spoiled brat of an animal. For that kind of thing I've got no use. No use at all. I've seen too many good horses ruined that way. But"—and the old man shook a finger—"but the most important thing about a horse, in my opinion, is getting its confidence. Getting it to trust you. Getting it to know that you won't ever ask it to do anything it shouldn't or couldn't do. Once you get that—then you and the horse are partners. Then you get things done, each relying on and believing in the other. That's a fine thing to see, a fine thing to be a part of. It doesn't happen often, more's the pity, but when it does, it is awfully rewarding. It's happened to me a few times. Maybe it can happen to you now."

The trainer stopped, considering things. "There may be times," he added, "especially at first, and once in a while for a refresher, that you'll have to be strict and stern, to show who's boss. Do it firmly, but don't do it brutally. Your voice is usually whip or reward enough. They know the tone. If you do it right, you won't have to do it often. Take your time with this colt, boy. Get its confidence. Get to be partners with it. Then you'll have something. Something really fine."

He slapped Rick quickly on the shoulder. "That's all I've got to say," he finished, "except good luck. And thank you. He's too good a colt not to have his chance. Now, let me see what sort of place you've got to keep him in till he gets over being homesick."

Rick led the way to the new stall. "Fine," Darwin Mears approved, "couldn't be better. Give him a little hay that he won't look at for a while, and keep an eye on him."

The truck and trailer moved off down the hill and the colt, by *Mon Oncle, out of the fine mare, Never Fear, had a new home, a new life, a new master.

Perhaps it really began that first night, the tie between the colt that would be gray, and the slim, serious-faced boy with the quiet hands and voice. On the other hand, perhaps it had been building all through the past weeks. But this was, suddenly, a new world to the young animal, with strange sounds, strange smells, strange lights and shadows, and there was no sheltering dam to get behind. There was just the big box stall of new lumber, with the shavings deep under foot. There was nothing that the youngster knew, or could recognize, or could trust except the figure of the boy there in the corner of the stall. And the small horse was too terrified to pay any attention to that for a long time.

Darkness came, and still there were the piercing shrill whinnies that shook the small body, the same frantic running about the stall. Kink came to the stable and looked through the three-inch openings between the stall boards above the four-foot-high kicking planks.

"You want some dinner?" he asked. Rick shook his head. "I'm going to stay with him," he said, "till he quiets, anyway."

"I'll bring you a sandwich," Kink said, disappearing from the light of the big overhead bulb. Kink brought the sandwich and left, saying nothing. And, after a while, curiosity began to calm the colt. Tenderloin helped.

Tenderloin's stall, which he could enter and leave as he desired, was next to the colt's. And, in the early night, the colt finally became aware of the wet muzzle pressed against the three-inch slits between the stalls, the gusty blowings that were almost a roar, as the big steer tried to see and smell what was going on beside him. Slowly the colt walked over to the black muzzle. Carefully he sniffed. Slowly he relaxed. Just a very little, but a little more every minute.

He seemed to become aware of Rick, sitting in a corner of the stall, his back against the planks. He went back to Tenderloin, sniffed again, long and lingeringly, snorted a small, short snort, and turned away. He picked up a bit of hay and brought it slowly over to Rick, his head outstretched, hoofs small and shining. His nose went over Rick's shirt, his hair, his face. Then he gave almost a little sigh, and ate the hay.

The sun was throwing its first shafts of light through the trees and across the dewy fields when Kink Ballou came down to the stable and found them. The boy was asleep, head low on his chest, slumped in the stall corner; the gangly colt was stretched on the shavings near him; the tomcat was in the boy's lap.

"The country," Kink Ballou thought to himself, "is a good place to raise a boy." He didn't wake them.

He picked up a bit of hay and brought it slowly over to Rick

Six

IN THE DAYS THAT FOLLOWED, RICK COAXED THE COLT
to drink the skimmed milk, diluted a bit with lime
water, that Lena Baird fixed for him. "Whole milk
would be too rich," she explained, "but this will make
him grow." He had crushed oats, too, with a little bran,
in his feed box.

After a week or so, when Suzi was there, they put
the halter on the colt and, lead shank on each side, took
him out and around the farm. That was an education.
He was quick and strong, this young one, now almost
four months old, and sometimes he nearly pulled the
pair off their feet as he dragged them, laughing, from
one new thing to another.

Abram delighted him. The colt ran at him, nuzzled
him, struck at him playfully, tried to romp with him as
a puppy would. Abram tolerated him, but retreated with
dignity. He sniffed Albert's tail feathers, making the
rooster leap high in horrified suprise, much to the ap-
parent cackling delight of his harem. He inspected the
old mare through her fence, but, surprisingly, showed
little interest in her thereafter. And, as the hot days of

August moved by, his devotion to, and dependence on, young Rick Ballou grew greater and greater.

Rick took him out alone now, on a long lead shank, wandering about the mowed fields with him, roaring in laughter as the unsuspected jump of a big grasshopper made the colt leap and play.

"I think I can let him go loose with me pretty soon," he said.

"Better be careful," Kink cautioned. "He could get into trouble before you could stop him."

But Rick felt that he could sense the right moment and, at the end of the month, he let the colt go loose one afternoon. For a minute the colt did not seem to realize that it was free. Then it moved a few steps, a few more, and then it ran. It ran across the big field, the bad leg wobbling, but the speed startling, and for a minute, Rick thought: "He's gone. I'll have a job catching him. He just wanted his freedom, that was all."

And then the gangling youngster turned, galloped back in haste to Rick, dropped its head, and grazed beside him. It was the last time the colt ever wore a lead shank on the farm. And it was the beginning of all the wonderful things—and of the great decision.

The first important discovery came on a hot, humid day, shortly after the colt first went loose. After lunch, Suzi rode up on Ulysses S. Grant. Rick and Kink were on the flagstoned terrace above the flower gardens. The colt grazed in the elm-tree shade beyond the post-and-rail fence that protected Kink's flowers. Suzi took the saddle and bridle off Ulysses. He and the colt exchanged sniffs and got along, plucking grass side by side. They knew each other.

"Hot," Kink said. "How about a swim?"

Suzi kept a faded suit at their house. When they had all changed, she said, "I'd better put Ulysses in a paddock. He might wander off home."

"Guess I'll let the young one come," Rick said. "He's never been to the pool."

The pool was a quarter of a mile away, through the hayfields and down a shaded woods road. The ground was damp and cool under their bare feet, the patches of sunlight bright through the trees. The colt followed along, walking, stopping to pluck a tempting leaf or two, trotting to catch up, always directly behind Rick. Rick loved the pool. It was a pond, really, with a curving dam of dirt, the sides of thick grass that they kept mowed like a lawn. It was a wonderful place to swim and relax, to lie in the shade or in the bright sunlight. The water lay clear, calm, and cool, spring-fed, two hundred feet across in a circle, deep, shelving off sharply. You could dive from the bank, and it was Rick's joy to run and throw himself far out in a stretching dive, landing with a great splash, coming up to the delicious coolness. He did that now, only this time it was different.

This time, as he surfaced, shaking the water from his head, there was a great whinnying, a frantic running back and forth on the wide dam, with tentative dashes, ankle-deep, into the water. The colt's eyes were never once off Rick, as he floated out in the center of the pond.

Suzi laughed delightedly, blowing water from her

The colt clambered up onto the bank

mouth as she paddled froglike. "He thinks you're drown-
ing," she called.

Rick swam in. "All right, fellow," he said, "all right."
He stood at the pond side, and the colt came to him,
nose down to the water, blowing at it, intrigued, but not
sure. This mirrorlike expanse was a brand new thing.

"I bet," Rick said, "that he'd like to swim. All horses
can swim. It would be fun. Can I take him in?"

Kink shook his head resignedly. "I knew it," he said.
"There goes my swimming privacy. By all means, take
him in. He's a member of the family. Don't mind me."
But he watched with interest as Rick, arms around the
colt's withers, tried to coax him into the water.

It took several efforts. The youngster would follow

He shook himself, the water flying

Rick in, ankle-deep, then knee-deep. Then he would whirl in fright, dash about the pond, tail high, stop, and then come back to Rick. The water fascinated him. Besides, it was cool. On the tenth trial he went in, belly-deep, took one more step with Rick beside him, and then had to swim as the water went deep.

He swam with his face flat in the water, like a dog, his withers and small rump barely above the surface, and Rick stayed with him, talking to him, encouraging him. They swam for perhaps thirty feet, swinging back to the bank, the colt clambering out and up onto the bank. Then he shook himself, the water flying, and then he went on a tear. He dashed over the turf, tail tucked low between his legs, tore through the open woods, in and out and back again, and finally, subsiding, back to Rick's side, cocky and very pleased with himself.

After that, in the days that followed, there was no keeping him from the water. The problem was, as Kink said ruefully, getting him to come out. Sometimes he would stand belly-deep in the water, and paw, first with one foot, then the other, the water flying in all directions. Then he would plunge his muzzle and nose in deep, up to his eyes, and blow delightedly. But mostly he swam, endlessly, tirelessly.

One Saturday after the colt had been to the pond a dozen times or more, when Rick had made his flying leap and surfaced, there was another greater splash near him. The colt had made his flying leap, too, landing ten feet away, snorting with pleasure.

"Hey," Rick said, "you be careful. You get big and do that, and you might be a problem." He had, at that moment, no idea how right he might be. Or why. But that came later. Kink brought up another matter one night as they were finishing a thick steak.

"You're going to have to pick out a name for this youngster of yours," he said, "something besides Buster or Fellow. Something that could be registered with the Jockey Club."

"Just what is the Jockey Club?" Rick inquired. "I really never have known, exactly."

"The association that keeps all the records on Thoroughbreds—ages, markings, racing records if any, breeding, get, everything."

"Oh," Rick said. "Well, you're good at names and things like that. Any suggestions?"

Kink had, it developed, given the matter considerable thought. "Yes," he admitted, "I do have an idea or two." He lit his pipe, blowing the blue smoke ceilingward. "You see, your colt has a French sire, *Mon Oncle. His dam's name is Never Fear. Now, there's a French phrase that was applied to some one of their kings, a long time ago, a phrase that has always been a pleasant and appealing one to me—*Sans peur et sans reproche*. It means, as every schoolboy should know, 'Without fear and without reproach, or blame.' This colt doesn't seem to have an ounce of fear in him—animals, thunder, lightning, cars, trucks, odd noises, certainly," —ruefully—"not water. So—may I make the suggestion that he be called Sans Peur?"

There was silence. Then Rick said, "But I can't always be saying 'whoa Sans Peur, stand Sans Peur.' It would be too long, too tongue-twisting, if you were in a hurry."

"Of course," Kink agreed, "naturally you wouldn't say that. Every horse, every Thoroughbred, has a stable name. A name you ordinarily use around him. You could call him San."

Rick considered the matter. "Yes," he said, "I think I like that. Sans Peur. Without fear. San. Thanks, Kink. I think you hit it."

Kink grinned. "I thought you'd like it. Matter of fact, I was so confident I had these made for you." He reached into a cupboard and brought out two thin boxes. Rick opened them.

The first was a slim brass halter plate for the cheek strap. In black cut letters was the name Sans Peur and, under that, in smaller type, the colt's sire and dam— *Mon Oncle—Never Fear. The other package was a larger plate, a stall plate, with the same lettering.

"Boy," Rick said, "they are slick." He grinned at Kink. "You were pretty sure, weren't you, that I'd go for that name?"

Kink nodded, only pleasantly perturbed. "Didn't think you could resist it," he admitted, "too perfectly descriptive."

Suddenly the grin faded from Rick's face.

"What's the matter?" Kink asked.

"Just one thing," Rick said, shaking his head, "just that I can't use either plate."

"And why not?" Kink demanded.

"Because," Rick explained, "one of the provisions Mr. Corcoran made when he gave me the colt was that I should never volunteer anything about his breeding. And this would certainly be volunteering something."

Kink stared at him unhappily. "Good grief," he said, "I never did think of that. You're right."

But Rick refused to be upset for long. "It really doesn't matter," he said, "you've picked a fine name for him, a wonderful name. Sans Peur." He repeated it slowly. "I hope he'll always be just that."

Seven

SCHOOL STARTED SHORTLY AFTER LABOR DAY. RICK WAS in high school now, in Woodville, a good forty-five minutes ride on the bus, but he did his chores every morning before going, leaving enough time to brush and handle San, and to let him out for a few minutes. In fact, if it was a minute or two after six o'clock when he got to the stable, the colt would shrill an insistent whinny.

"A man can't even sleep around here any more," Kink said ruefully.

Kink was away a great deal that fall with commissions in the Middle West, so Mrs. Amyott spent many nights at the farm. She was completely sympathetic to the colt and Rick, so sympathetic that she even approved of a system for studying that Rick inaugurated.

He did not get home until well after four, and that left only an hour to romp with San before darkness and before the colt had to go into his stall. So, after dinner, Rick took a lamp on a long cord to the stable, set up a box for a desk, and did his homework there, with San loose on the floor. The system pleased San, who could wander outside, come back in, nudge his partner, disturb the papers, and, once, knock over the desk. It was not, however, a system conducive to concentration, and Kink put an abrupt end to it when he came back from a trip.

"Sorry," he said firmly, "work is work. You do it in your room where you can concentrate. First year high school is too important to tamper with."

"But San ought to get out more," Rick remonstrated. "The more he uses that leg, the better for it, Jim Robbins says."

"I don't care if he's loose, or what," Kink said, "but you work in your room."

The next night Rick had been at work in his ground-floor room for half an hour or so, when there was a barely audible brushing against the window pane at his shoulder, and a soft whinny. San was peering in at him. Rick slid the sash up.

"Quiet, San," he whispered with severe affection, "don't make a noise or you'll have to go back to your stall." The colt moved away and began cropping the dead grass. At nine-thirty, two hours later, he was still not far from the window. Rick walked him down and shut him in the stall.

Every evening after that, as soon as the light went on in Rick's room, the gray colt was waiting outside.

As October and then November rolled on, bringing down the leaves, stripping the trees bare to the low moaning winds, Rick added corn to the oats and bran diet, keeping up the skimmed milk and lime water. The colt was growing fast. The weekends that he and Rick and, often Suzi, spent wandering through the back hills, carrying their lunch in a shoulder roll, had strengthened and developed the young animal.

"I think the swimming helped too," Suzi said.

"Do you really think his leg is better?" Rick demanded.

"I do," she said stoutly, "and the rest of him is just magnificent."

Rick didn't see Suzi so often now. She was still in the country grade school, and would be for another year. He missed her, but high school was a busy new life.

Jim Robbins, the veterinarian, came to the farm one Saturday in early December. "He'll be a real steel-gray, once he sheds out come spring," he said, looking the colt over. "Trot him around, will you?" He watched the off hind leg keenly.

"A lot better, really a lot," he affirmed. "I think it's coming, Rick. He's in top condition. You're doing a good job." Rick glowed.

"Give him as much exercise as you can this winter," Jim said, climbing into his jeep, "only watch it when there's ice."

Christmas came, and the Bairds sent up a bushel basket of carrots for San and for the other animals. Rick gave San a new halter for the one he had outgrown. And Kink gave Rick a beautiful bridle, with laced hunting reins and a light snaffle bit. "You won't be using this for a while," he said, "but it'll be ready."

Two days after Christmas he said to Rick, "By the way, San's birthday will be on January first."

"No," Rick said, shaking his head, "he was born in April—the seventeenth."

Kink corrected him. "All Thoroughbreds," he said, "are one year old on the first of January following their birth. That's for racing purposes, and it's official for all of them, which is why an early colt is bigger than one born later in the spring or summer."

"Well," Rick conceded, "if you say so." He brightened. "We'll have a party for him on his birthday."

They had it in the stable. The snow came down softly and quietly over the bleak hills and meadows outside. There was no cake, but there was a great tub of cut-up apples and carrots, barely sweetened with a touch of the Bairds' maple syrup. Tenderloin and Rose of Washington Square each had a feed pail in their stalls, with Abram and San loose on the barn floor. Suzi rode up on Ulysses S. Grant. Thomas Jefferson Tibbs purred over a plate of meat. Albert and his harem enjoyed cracked corn. Peace reigned among the animals.

Kink had a keg of cider on a deal table on the barn floor, with a great bowl of crisply warm sugar dougnuts from Mrs. Amyott's oven. She brought her nephew and his little boy, aged five, who was constantly under the animals' feet and miraculously unstepped upon. Tom and Lena Baird came in the truck. Three or four other neighbors admired San, then sat down to gossip on the benches against the wall.

Darwin Mears arrived and perched on the grain bin, quietly looking over the colt. Even Slade Corcoran appeared, big, gracious, just a little too pleasant to everybody. He scarcely glanced at the gray colt, but talked with Kink at one side. And Kink was nervous, with something on his mind.

After half an hour he disappeared into the tack room. When he came out, he was carrying a paper-covered package. As he stood beside the deal table, people stopped talking and looked at him.

"This probably isn't very good," he said, half apologetically, "but I . . . well, I had some fun doing it, and I thought maybe Ricky here would like it in the years to come. And that you, our friends, might like to see it now."

He raised the paper that protected the two-foot-square canvas, and Rick caught his breath quickly. Mrs. Amyott said, "My isn't that wonderful," and Slade Corcoran moved up to the painting.

It was a head of San, done in pastels, with all the detail of the colt's baby head, the broad, concave forehead, the velvet muzzle, the questioning, not quite sure look in the youngster's eyes—the look that had caught Rick's heart.

"That's really excellent, Kink," Slade Corcoran said, "I didn't know that you did animals."

"I don't," Kink said. "This is the first time. Just in the family." The others crowded around.

"It's terrific, Kink," Rick said at his father's side, his glance trying to say just how much the painting, and the thought behind it, meant to him.

Darwin Mears slid down from the grain bin. "I'd like to propose a toast," he said, his cider glass held

"I'd like to propose a toast"

high, "a toast to these good people, Kink and Rick, and to his colt, Sans Peur." He paused. "May the years that come," he continued, "be even better."

The glasses were raised and voices said "Hear, Hear," and the gray colt ate his apples and carrots, paying no attention.

"But not too much better," Rick whispered to himself.

The party broke up after a while. It had been fun and the painting was wonderful. But somehow there was something in the thought of the future that frightened Rick. Something seemed to lurk there that threatened the bond between him and San. He did not know what that something was, of course, but, deep inside, he had a feeling that such a finely bred, handsome animal might not be really his, might be with him only temporarily, as a loan. Winter is a waiting time on the farm, a time when thoughts like those could come back again and again.

Kink believed that animals should get outdoors in all kinds of weather, so he had invented a swinging door, framed in a thickness of canvas-covered foam rubber, so that the door would swing itself shut tight to keep the stall warm, and could be pushed open by an eager nose. Tenderloin and Rose each had such a door leading from their stalls to their paddocks, and Kink made another for San. Abram had the run of the barn floor and didn't need one.

The snow fascinated the young horse. He pawed at it frantically, buried his nose in it, rolled in it, and raced around, throwing up great clouds of the feathery stuff.

On weekends Rick took him on long walks through the woods and open fields, the colt loose. Whenever there was a thaw and the snow became heavy and apt to cake on the colt's feet, Rick would rub butter all over the inside of San's hoofs to keep the snow from balling up there and twisting an ankle.

"Darn expensive way to keep a horse's feet snow-free," Kink grumbled, when Rick disappeared with another quarter pound.

And then, almost overnight, it was spring, and Sans Peur was really twelve months old, really a yearling.

Eight

APRIL IS NOT THE BEST MONTH IN VERMONT. IT OFTEN
snows, the trees are still gaunt skeletons, the mud
is not always gone. Nevertheless, there is promise of
better things. Some days are, as the farmers' wives say,
like a good apple pie: "warm in the middle and crisp
around the edges." Cows are rough-coated in barnyards.
Horses are shaggy, wandering in the fields searching
for early blades of grass. Wild animals come out of winter quarters, looking for food, exploring. San learned
about one of these animals the hard way.

It was early morning, at the end of the month, the
sun bright, but the air chilly. San roamed about the
barnyard and to the wooded edges of the meadow beyond. Suddenly Rick, doing barn chores, heard him snort
loudly. There was the quick sound of a hoof pounding,
then the snort again. Rick went to the big barn door.

The colt was fifty yards away, at the fringe of woods.
His nose was down, and he seemed to be pushing at
something. Rick caught a quick glimpse of what it was.
"San," he yelled, "San, come here! Out of that!" He was
too late.

The small black and white animal that San was

prodding with an inquisitive nose had had enough. It turned its back to San, and, suddenly, the big colt was shaking his head, rubbing his face against a foreleg, moving frantically as the skunk, tail high, retreated majestically to the woods. The colt turned finally, hurrying back to Rick, still shaking its head dejectedly.

"Serves you right," Rick said, and then, as the colt came close, "Good grief! Get away from me, San. Get away. You reek."

The colt did reek. Albert came around a corner of the barn, stopped, cackled frantically to the hens and herded them away. Abram came near, shook his long ears in disgust, vanished hurriedly. Thomas Jefferson Tibbs put his ears back, lashed with his tail, and disappeared, glowering, up the ladder to the mow.

Rick retreated toward the house. The colt followed him, appealing, cowed. Mrs. Amyott came to the back door, sniffed, and said, "Goodness gracious, Ricky, you'll have to put him in his stall. We just can't have him here now. After breakfast we'll see what can be done."

Rick managed to herd San into his stall and then

Bottle after bottle of tomato juice was rubbed in

retired, gasping for air. The colt was utterly subdued, standing head down, eyeing Rick hopefully through the openings between the stall boards. After breakfast Suzi came up on Ulysses S. Grant.

"Tomato juice," she said. "You sort of wash them in tomato juice. Our dog, Lady, gets into skunks, and that's what we do."

"But a horse," Mrs. Amyott demurred, "is pretty big . . ."

"Kink just bought a new case before he went to Chicago," Rick remembered. "It's some special kind, but it'll do."

Fortunately the day turned warm. The colt stood on the barn floor, stained a dark red as bottle after bottle of tomato juice was rubbed into his coat. Kink got home late that afternoon. "A whole case!" he exclaimed in irritation. "Did you have to use all twelve bottles?"

"Well, he's a big colt," Rick said, apologetically, "but it did the job. Smell him."

"Thank you," Kink said, retreating, "I'll take your word for it." He shook his head. "No swim, no sleep, no tomato juice." But he looked the colt over appreciatively. "He *is* getting big, isn't he?"

"Almost fifteen hands," Rick said proudly. "Darwin Mears was up to see him and measured him with the stick. Mr. Mears says he'll go close to seventeen hands when he's full grown."

The colt really grew that summer, while some important things were happening. The first, and most important, was the strengthening of the bond, the interdependence and deep affection between the lanky, tow-headed boy and the steel-gray colt, an affection that brought a sudden lump to Kink's throat as he watched them together throughout the summer.

In the early morning, after chores and breakfast, with the mist still heavy in the valley pockets, Rick would be in the barnyard, the colt standing stock still without lead shank or halter, while Rick brushed his coat to a gleam, fluffed out the black tail and mane, and cleaned out the hoofs. The colt had learned to lift up each hoof as Rick reached for it, and to hold it up while Rick picked it clean. Every five weeks or so, the blacksmith came and rasped the hoofs level. San did not, as yet, wear shoes.

After the grooming, the pair would often wander off into the back hills, Rick with his .22 rifle, hunting for woodchucks. If Rick saw the chuck first, off in a field, he would say "Stand!" firmly to San, and the colt learned to obey and remain motionless until Rick sighted and fired. In time, San learned to look for the pests himself, and would often stop and stand before Rick even saw their quarry. They killed woodchucks because the animals ruined crops and left deep, dangerous holes where a horse or a cow could easily break a leg. The gunfire bothered San at first, but he soon became used to it, not moving a muscle as the gun went off beside him. He was not a good companion at all sports, however. At fishing, for example, he was useless.

"Any luck?" Kink inquired one evening when Rick returned with rod and creel and colt. Rick shook his head disgustedly.

"With him?" he demanded, nodding at San. "I wondered why I wasn't getting a bite in the good pools, and then I discovered this monkey here, a hundred yards ahead of me, wading in every pool, even rolling in some, scaring every fish for miles around. I don't take him fishing any more. Besides, when a horse fly gets on a spot where he can't reach, he comes tearing through the brush to get me to kill it for him. A pest. Just a pest." The gray colt stood by, delighted.

It was at the pond that Rick and San and Suzi had their best times. It wasn't long before the colt was towing them about the pond as they clung to his withers.

Sometimes he dove under them, coming up to lift them out of the water amid shouts and screams. On really hot days they spent whole afternoons in the water, with breaks of lying on the grassy banks in the sun, San grazing and drying off nearby.

The days flew by so fast, there were so many things to do, that it was August before Rick fully realized what had happened to San.

Tom Baird spoke of it first. "He doesn't limp any more, that you can notice, and the hock stays straight in line. Wouldn't scarcely know which leg had been off."

Dr. Robbins confirmed it. "I thought it would take a year," he said, examining the colt. "I don't know if it was the hill work, the good feeding, or what. Probably a combination."

"And the swimming," Suzi added, looking trim in her levis, her pug nose deeply freckled.

"That's right," Robbins agreed, "swimming's great for strengthening and tightening muscles. Anyway, he moves sound. And," he said, admiringly, "he sure is in shape. I've seldom seen such a well-developed horse at his age."

San was truly a magnificent creature. His head was small, forehead concave, eyes bright and prominent, ears small, quick moving, curved in at the tips. His neck was beautiful, slim at the throat with a curving line deepening to a great chest that spread broad and strong. He had high withers, and the angle of his shoulder was perfect. The forearm was strong, already deep-muscled,

San was truly a magnificent creature

and the bone in his lower leg, the cannon, was wide and thick. The angle of his pasterns promised a velvet-smooth ride.

He was, as the saying goes, "deep through the heart," a great chest developing, the rib cage sprung wide and strong, the back short enough, the quarters already deep-ridged with muscle from the hill work, denoting tremendous power. His tail set in at just the right angle, but the thing that brought all the parts together, and that made you stop and stare, was the combination of fineness and strength, the quiet dignity that the youngster already possessed, the poise, the confidence, and the pride.

"Sans Peur," Rick would say, looking at him, "you don't know what fear is."

Slade Corcoran heard about him, of course. And one afternoon in late August the Jaguar swung up the hill.

Kink was away that afternoon, and Rick and San had just come back from the pond. They were relaxing, Rick in a chair on the terrace, San grazing in the meadow that was growing back to rowen, or second-crop hay. The long, low, yellow car growled hoarsely up the hill, then stopped, as Slade Corcoran climbed stiffly out. He was in jodhpurs as usual, with a light shirt, and a white linen cap at a careful angle.

"Hello, Ricky," he said, his small eyes looking only at the colt, "hot, isn't it?"

"Yes, sir," Rick said, suddenly wary, and vaguely fearful. "Won't you sit down, sir?"

Corcoran walked slowly over to the gray, examining him carefully, thoroughly. The colt raised his head and gazed at this new man unconcernedly.

"Go on," Slade Corcoran said suddenly, "move. Run around." He made a motion as if he had a whip in his hand. San did not move, but stood there silently, appraisingly.

"Make him step out, will you," Corcoran said irritably. Rick ran with the reluctant youngster, getting him into a trot, then a canter, then into a playful gallop across the meadow. The big man tipped his white cap back on his forehead and watched them. Rick came back, panting. There was silence.

"He seems sound enough," Corcoran said finally.

"Yes sir," Rick said. "We—we think he is."

"You've done a fine job with him, Ricky," Corcoran went on, almost too pleasantly, too admiringly. "I wouldn't have thought it possible. But then, there probably wasn't anything basically wrong with him."

"He certainly was awfully lame, sir," Rick managed, the fear mounting inside him. Corcoran waved a hand.

"Yes, but he's magnificent now. As perfect a yearling as I've seen around." He paused, and his white teeth gleamed at Rick. "Really," he continued, "much too fine a Thoroughbred to be wasting his time playing around a farm. Even," and the smile broadened, "with such fine companions as you and young Suzi Baird. And these quaint creatures"—with a wave at Abram and Tenderloin in the background. "A horse this fine should be where he belongs—in the big time. Don't you agree, son?"

Rick tried to clear his throat, and the words came out shakily. "He—he's happy here, sir. He's having a good time."

Slade Corcoran waved his hand again. "I'm sure he is," he said. "I think it's been just the spot for him. Wonderful. But"—and he turned the smile on again—"let's be realistic, you and I, shall we? Let's admit I made a mistake. You have to pay for your mistakes."

He leaned toward Rick, trying to be man to man. "Look, Ricky," he said, "suppose we say that I'll give you one hundred dollars a month for the board and care you've given this colt. Let's say I pay you fifteen hun-

74

dred dollars for all the trouble and expense you've been to. How would that strike you?"

Rick stood there, stricken, feeling the back of his neck begin to shake the way it did when he was frightened and getting mad. "And then what, sir?" he managed.

"And then," Slade Corcoran said smoothly, "then I take the colt back where he belongs to get him ready for the racing life he's been bred to—that he's meant for. That's his heritage. Thoroughbreds are born to run, Ricky. You know that."

"This one isn't, Mr. Corcoran," Rick said. "He belongs to me and—and he likes it here. It's his home now."

The heavy man with the red jowls looked at him hard, measuring him. "Suppose we said two thousand dollars." He spoke evenly, ingratiatingly.

Rick shook his head, the blood pounding in his face. "No, sir," he said.

Slade Corcoran raised an eyebrow. "You know," he said too pleasantly, "you know, I suppose, I could just take him. I don't think you have any papers, any bill of sale." He smiled, his teeth very white, and got into his car. The motor backfired as he drove down the hill, his hand up in a slight wave as he vanished around the turn.

The look on Rick's face frightened Kink when he got home before dinner. The boy's jaw was set tight, his lips were a thin straight line, his eyes were narrow, glinting slits.

"What happened to you?" Kink demanded.

Rick told him, the words coming out sharply and harshly. "Can he take him?" he asked.

Kink hesitated. "I don't know," he admitted. "Who was there when he said you could have the colt?"

"Darwin Mears and Jim Robbins," Rick said. "They'll know."

"They also work for Slade," Kink said drily. "But after dinner I might have a talk with them."

"Can I go with you?" Rick asked.

Kink shook his head. "The way you're feeling, I think you'd better keep out of it for a while."

At seven-thirty Kink drove into Darwin Mears' yard. Mears, a bachelor, lived in a small red cottage on the edge of the Bellemead land. As Kink went through the gate in the white picket fence, he could see the old man sitting in a chair, reading a newspaper. He got up slowly at Kink's knock, peering over his glasses, his slippers shuffling as he came to the open door. A large cat watched, yellow-eyed, from a padded chair.

Kink told his story, and the manager heard him out, with no interruptions. Then he filled his pipe carefully.

"The boy's right," he said, tamping the tobacco. "Mr. Corcoran told him he could have the colt, provided he kept it out of Corcoran's sight and never volunteered anything about his breeding."

"Would you repeat that, publicly, if you were asked?" Kink said.

Darwin Mears regarded him, wide-eyed. "Why not?" he asked. "I was there. I heard it."

Kink hesitated. "I only meant," he said, somewhat lamely, "that you work for Slade, and that perhaps . . ." He left the sentence unfinished.

Mears smiled bleakly. "And that perhaps he might fire me," he finished. A match flared at his pipe and he puffed blue smoke. "I think, Mr. Ballou," he said, "that Mr. Corcoran needs me more than I need him. I've made him some money over the years and, if he shouldn't need me, I've some of it tucked away. Besides, I'd have to live with myself."

Kink got up. "Thank you," he said, putting out his hand, "I hope I don't have to call on you, but I appreciate your willingness."

The old man nodded, and, as Kink started off, added with a quick gleam in his eyes, "I sure would love to see that gray youngster run, though. He could be awfully good." Then he went back to his paper, stopping to run a hand over the big cat that had not moved.

Jim Robbins said the same thing, while three young children played under the maples in his front yard. "It's Rick's colt," he said. "I heard the whole thing."

"Bellemead must be a big part of your practice," Kink said.

Robbins' face went serious. "It is," he said, "I'd hate to lose it. But I'd hate to keep it—under certain conditions."

When Kink Ballou left Dr. Robbins, it was a little after nine o'clock, and Kink made a quick decision. It was just half an hour later when he drove his car through the gates to Bellemead and up the long, winding avenue between the stretching lengths of white board fence, ghostly in the darkness.

The house was long, two-storied, slate-roofed, of old, pinkish brick, the portico high with its white pillars. A houseman answered the bell. Mr. Corcoran was at home. He would tell Mr. Corcoran. Returning, the man led Kink to a small library, the shelves ceiling-high. Slade Corcoran, in a maroon velvet jacket, dark trousers, gleaming patent leather pumps, rose from a leather chair, the ice rattling as he put down a glass.

"Kink," he said, "how nice. Sit down. Drink?"

"Thank you, no," Kink said. He hesitated. Slade Corcoran rushed on, almost too pleasantly.

"Well," he said, "hear you're doing big things. Signed up to do Betsy Holmeyer. Great girl, Betsy. Loaded with money. But homely. Very homely. You can take care of that, though, eh Kink." He winked, going to the sideboard to mix a drink. "Sure you won't join me?"

Kink shook his head. "Well," Slade Corcoran said, sitting down and showing his even, white teeth, "what can I do for you? Or you for me?" He waited.

Kink examined the knuckles of his hands. Then he looked at Slade. "Probably not much of anything, Slade, beyond what you've already done. Actually, I came here just to correct a misapprehension on Rick's part. I told Rick that I was sure, absolutely sure, that a man of your position in the neighborhood and community, in the whole state, in fact, would never change his mind about something as important as what you told him that day when he and Darwin Mears and Jim Robbins were with you in the foaling barn. It was the day you were discussing what to do with the lame colt. I told him that you knew the animal was his—Rick's—and that all you wanted to do, now or any time, was what was best for the colt and for Rick and for everybody. In other words, I told him that you had no idea of taking the colt away from him."

There was silence—not a long silence, but long enough for the wheels of thought to whirl. Then Slade Corcoran beamed, waving a hand. Kink had given him his out, his excuse. He took it.

"Of course," he said, "of course that was all I wanted to do—what was, and is, best for the colt, and, naturally, for Rick. I thought, and still do, that the colt should race. As I told Rick, that's what he was bred for. He shouldn't be denied his heritage, his purpose in life. He's as fine a prospect as ever came from Bellemead or anywhere else. It's a shame he shouldn't have his chance. That's the way I feel. I offered to pay well. I'm prepared to make any other reasonable arrangement."

"But—" and he waved the soft hand again—"if Ricky doesn't agree with me, if he wants to keep the colt as— as just a pet, a sort of decorative companion, why that's up to him. That's his decision. I hope he makes the right one. I repeat, though, that it's his to make."

Slade Corcoran had wriggled clear. He knew it. Kink Ballou knew it. Kink got up. "I was sure that was the way you would feel, Slade," he said, "and I'm sorry to have disturbed you so late in the evening. Thanks for setting matters straight." He moved to the door. Slade followed him.

"I'll tell you, though," he said, "that I'm going to keep after Ricky to race the colt. He's too good to waste. Can't blame me, can you?" He beamed again, putting out his hand. Kink took it.

"No," he said, "I can't blame anyone, ever, for his feelings."

Rick Ballou slept the sleep of the exhausted that night, after his father had come home and talked with him. But, before his eyes finally closed, the words, as Kink had repeated them to him carefully, ran through his mind over and over again. ". . . shouldn't be denied his heritage. Bred to run . . . as fine a prospect . . . he could be good, awfully good."

"I won't do it," he muttered, turning fitfully under the sheet. "I won't. He loves it here. He and I." The gray colt stood outside the boy's window and, finally, lay down in the meadow beyond and slept there.

Nine

THAT WAS A GOOD FALL, WITH THE COLT COMING TWO, the partridge hunting, and the new house—or the addition to the old one.

On the last weekend in September Kink had his shotguns out in the kitchen, cleaning them. "Bird season opens tomorrow," he said to Rick. "Do you want to go out?" They both enjoyed hunting partridge in season because, as Kink said, it was one kind of hunting that required real skill, and where the game had more than an even chance.

"Sure," Rick said, "I think we'd love it."

Kink looked at him. "We?" he queried.

Rick grinned, embarrassed. "Yes," he said, "San and I. Now wait—" as Kink tried to break in—"you may think this is silly, but I've taken him woodchuck hunting a lot, and he's quiet, stands when and where I tell him, and often sees or smells them long before I do. Horses have an acute sense of smell and sight, you know. San often moves along with his nose to the ground, scenting, and, well, I just think he might develop into something pretty unusual—a horse that could find and flush up birds. Anyway, it would be fun to try it, don't you think?" His face was quite red. Kink shook his head slowly, wonderingly.

"Now," he said, "I have heard everything. A horse as a bird dog." He shook his head again.

"Well," Rick said, "you haven't had a bird dog since Bartlett died, three years ago. Will you give it a try? Just to see what happens?"

Kink, finishing the gun, spread his hands in surrender. "I'll try anything once," he said.

And so the opening morning of the partridge season saw one of the most unusual bird-hunting groups ever to set forth into the fields and woods—a father, a son, and a large, still slightly gangly, eager-eyed gray horse, on an utterly unnecessary shank and halter.

San was not an immediate success as a finder and indicator of birds. But he did stand on command and he did not flinch at gunfire. After five or six days in the field, when several birds had been shown to him, and he had been allowed to nose and smell them, he began to get the idea.

After two weeks of hunting they let him loose in the back meadows, now growing up to popple and evergreens. When three weeks more had passed, he would work his way slowly through the country, nose down, not ranging far and fast like a dog, but moving slowly, methodically, searchingly. When he stopped and raised his head, he did not, of course, point. But he did stand stock-still, eyes straight at his quarry, until the birds were flushed and roared away. Then, after the guns had fired, he would drop his head and, muzzle to the ground, would search out the dead birds, nosing them carefully.

"I never thought it could happen," Kink admitted in November, "but give him another season or two and he'll be *almost* as useful as a dog."

Cold weather came early that winter, and, with it, an idea that Rick had been waiting to bring up. The first snowfall—six inches of soft powder—drifted gently down through the early December night. In the morning San was outside Rick's window, snow clinging to his back and mane, and there was a large spot of melted snow on the ground where he had slept.

"For Pete's sake," Kink said, "has that horse been out there all night? Why didn't you put him in his stall?" Rick kept busy with the eggs on the stove. "Do you want him to freeze?" Kink continued.

"No," Rick said, still not looking up, "but he likes it there. And I like to have him there. He's been sleeping, or grazing, outside my window at night most of the summer." There was silence as he put the eggs on plates.

When Rick sat down, he said, "There's something I'd like to ask you, if—if you won't think it's crazy."

Kink stirred his coffee. "Go ahead," he said. "After what you two have done already, I'm prepared for anything."

"Well," Rick said, slowly and carefully, "it's kind of like having your dog sleep in your room, the way Bartlett did with you. I don't mean," he went on hurriedly, as Kink raised a horrified face, "that San would sleep in my room. But"—and he hesitated again—"I thought that perhaps we could have a sort of lean-to built out there, outside my room, with one of those marvelous weather-tight doors that you invented for the stable, and then San could sleep right there, and I could leave my window open, and—well—that would be that. Do you see what I mean?" He looked at his father helplessly, pleadingly. "Do you think it's crazy?" he said.

"Certainly," Kink said, "certainly I think it's crazy. But"—he drank some coffee slowly, and Rick watched him spellbound, hopefully—"but as Lena said, it's the things that sometimes seem a little crazy, the things that are different, unusual, that make life worth living, that give it bubble and excitement. If we didn't do some of those things, life could get pretty humdrum. Nothing new. Look what happened to painting. However, just to be mildly practical on this particular matter, wouldn't this houseside stall make things, er, just a bit ripe at times?"

Rick shook his head, all enthusiasm now. "No," he said, "that's another thing I meant to tell you. I've been working on that for quite a while now, and it's coming fine."

"What is?" Kink frowned.

"Well," Rick explained, "I got reading about how they housebreak horses and other big animals for the theater, television, things like that, and that it wasn't so difficult, really. So I've been training San, because it meant I'd have one less stall to pick up. And he's caught on. He's foolproof—almost—now." He looked at his father, delighted.

"And," Kink said, nodding, "and because you had

this stall-by-your window idea in the back of your head all the time. I get it." Rick grinned sheepishly. Kink pushed back his chair.

"Rick," he said, "I'm not a nature faker. Neither are you. I don't believe in attributing qualities or abilities to animals that they never can have. San's a horse. You're a human. But . . ." He looked down at the boy, and the look told how proud he was of him. Then he went on. "But there's some communication between you and this horse, some special bond, and it's a fine thing. A wonderful thing, I think. You go ahead and get Bill Kenyon to put up that stall and the swinging door before San gets pneumonia." He gave Rick's shoulder a quick slap, and disappeared into his room.

Bill Kenyon, the carpenter, may have had his own thoughts about the job, when Rick called him, but he had the stall built in ten days. He carried the roof line of the house out for twelve feet, ran it the length of Rick's room—about eighteen feet—put in a clay floor, and installed the swinging door with the tight-fitting foam rubber and canvas frame. Rick put a deep layer of clean shavings in the stall.

"Might as well just take out my glass window sash, top and bottom, Mr. Kenyon," he said. "We won't need it."

Bill Kenyon finished the job and drove off in his truck, looking straight ahead, a blank expression on his face.

"Martha," he said to his wife that night, "that's probably the smartest and best-looking young horse I ever saw in my life. He just stood there most all the time I was building that stall against the house, and when I was through he just walked in. Almost seemed to thank me. Maybe Kink Ballou and Rick do some funny things, but, man, what I wouldn't give to be that boy's age and have an animal like that."

"Eat your dinner, Bill," his wife told him. "You did enough things when you were a boy, a lot more foolish than that. You want I should remind you of some of them?"

"Never mind," Bill Kenyon said hastily, reaching for the gravy.

The gray colt slept outside the boy's window now. It was warm in his stall and, in the early morning, he would put his head through the window and waken his friend. At night he seemed to enjoy watching Rick work over his studies under the lamp. He became very neat.

Rick was a sophomore at high school, and, after the first of the year, Sans Peur was a two-year-old, entering his third year.

"They start racing horses as two-year-olds," Rick told himself. "I wonder if that's what I should be doing with San? If that's what he would really like to do? Instead of being around here—with me." The thought kept coming back to him again and again, keeping him awake sometimes at night, troubling him.

"I'll go over," he said to himself, "and talk to Darwin Mears." But he kept putting it off.

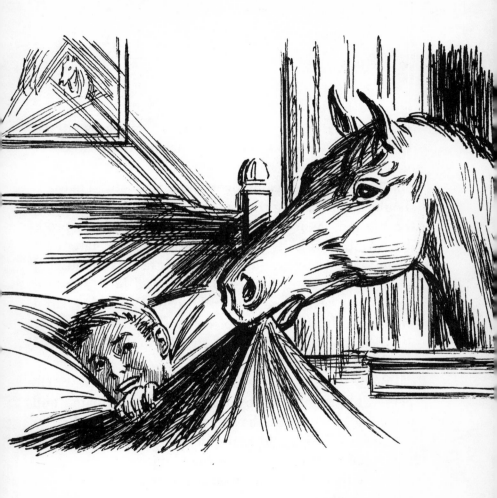

He would put his head through the window and waken his friend

Ten

BY MAY THE WEATHER WAS WARM, THE GRASS TRYING to fight its way to greenery through the dead cover of winter.

Slade Corcoran came over one afternoon. "That colt should be in training right now," he muttered, watching the big gray as it wandered about the barnyard, prodding Albert with its muzzle, scattering the harem. "I never saw a two-year-old develop this fast. He's muscled up a year ahead of himself already, and he'll grow for three more." He turned abruptly to Rick. "You've had a saddle and bridle on him, of course," he demanded.

Rick shook his head. "No, sir," he said. "I thought I would this summer."

"Well, you should have," Corcoran said irritably. He peered at the colt. "Why don't you have a name and breeding plate on his halter, like any Thoroughbred?"

"Because," Rick told him quietly, "you said I couldn't volunteer anything about his breeding."

"Ridiculous," Slade Corcoran snorted. "I'll send over a halter plate."

"I have one," Rick said. "If you say it's all right, I'll put it on."

"Of course put it on," Corcoran said. "Have you registered his name and so forth with the Jockey Club?"

"No, sir," Rick said.

"Well, get it done," Corcoran said, climbing into his car. "I'll write for the papers to fill in. You just might get some sense and want to race him. I'm still hoping he gets his chance." He gunned the Jaguar down the driveway, scattering gravel.

Rick had his driving license now and, early in June, he drove the jeep, top off, windshield turned down rakishly, over to Darwin Mears' place. The manager wasn't home, but Rick found him at the practice track, watching an exercise boy working a two-year-old. When the boy walked the horse back to the stable, Rick told Mears what was worrying him. The old man leaned against the track fence and heard him out.

"He just might be a famous horse," Rick ended, "like Man O' War or Native Dancer. I wouldn't want to deny him that. I just don't know."

Mears considered the distant landscape. Then he said, "How old are you, son?"

"Sixteen," Rick told him.

"Well," Darwin Mears said slowly, "you'll have a lot of decisions to make in your lifetime. You might as well start right now. Nobody but you can decide this. He's your horse and I'm afraid it's your problem."

"But"—and he turned to look at the boy beside him, growing up now, wide-shouldered, strong through the neck and chest—"one thing I will tell you. *Don't* race him *now*, as a two-year-old. Too many owners"—with a

89

glance toward the big brick house—"are in a hurry. A two-year-old just isn't developed, not even a special horse like this San, or whatever you call him. His bones haven't hardened, he hasn't really muscled up, he isn't ready for strain. And the tracks today are hard. The public is speed-crazy, record-crazy. Oh, the running surface looks soft enough, after the harrow has scratched it up, but underneath it's hard. It ruins a young horse's legs. Have you ever seen a race-horse hospital?"

Rick shook his head. "Don't," Darwin Mears advised him, "not if you want to sleep well. It's full of youngsters with their legs pin-fired, tendons bowed, bones broken in their feet and legs. Whatever you finally decide, give him another year. That's all the advice I can give you."

The boy was so preoccupied, he barely remembered to say thanks as he turned away. "Well," he was thinking, "we'll have this summer anyway. A lot could happen this summer."

At the Baird Farm, Rick turned in. Tom Baird was working on his hay baler, getting ready for the two hundred or more tons of hay he would cut, cure, and stow in the big barns. Suzi was in the background.

"Mr. Baird," Rick said, after watching the work silently for a few minutes, "I wonder if you could use me as a hand three or four days a week. I can get things done around our place in three days, and I don't want to just hang around the rest of the time."

Tom Baird finished tightening a nut on the machine. "Always can use an extra hand haying," he said. "How about the first four days in the week?"

"Fine," Rick said. Suzi had taken it all in. She was fourteen now, and curves were beginning to appear. She would go to high school the next fall.

"I'm going to start breaking San to saddle and bridle," Rick said, going over to her. "Do you want to give me a hand the first time?"

"Sure," Suzi said eagerly. "Gee, I'm glad you're going to help out here, Rick."

She could, Rick thought, be real pretty if her nose wasn't always shiny and her hair stringy. "We can start in a day or so," he said, getting into the jeep and roaring the motor. "See you." He drove off, taking the corner too fast, being very nonchalant.

Suzi didn't help him with the colt in a day or so. Something happened to change that plan and, in a way, to change Suzi.

There was a girl in Rick's class at Woodville High, a blond girl named Cissy Parlance. She was small, trim-waisted, and her almost white hair came down in a straight sheen to her shoulders, and then curled under, smooth and gleaming. Her eyes were dark under long, dark lashes, and she would open them very wide and look up at Rick as if she thought he was wonderful. Rick had danced with her at the gym parties, and she used a perfume that was sharp and sweet and made him come back. Twice they had gone to the movies, with sodas afterward.

"You've got a license now," she said, just before school closed, "and your father lets you take the jeep. I want to see this wonderful horse you have out at your place."

"I'll drive you out," he said eagerly.

The day after he had talked with Tom Baird and Suzi, he picked Cissy up in Woodville, very trim in yellow shorts and a clinging, sleeveless blouse. He drove fast in the open jeep, and the wind was cool in their faces. Friends on the sidewalk waved, and it was all gay and fun.

"Want to stop at the crossroads for a coke?" he said, as they neared the farm, and Cissy nodded.

The crossroads store at Parnell Center had a big porch in front. It was cool and dim inside, smelling of rope and ginger. Over at one side there were some stools in front of a soft-drink bar. Suzi was sitting on one of the stools, about to sip orangeade from the bottle in her hands. There was a smooch of grease across one cheek, her blue blouse was faded and had a patch at one shoulder, and her boots were scuffed and worn. She had been working. Her eyes went big when she saw them, and the color crept up brightly in her neck and cheeks.

"Hi, Suzi," Rick said. "Suzi Baird, this is Cissy Parlance."

"Hi," Cissy said, looking at the list of soft drinks over the counter, one hand smoothing her blond hair. There was silence.

"Suzi," Rick said finally, "is going to be a freshman next year."

Cissy continued with the list and the smoothing. "How exciting," she said, not looking at Suzi.

*Suzi was sitting on one of the stools, about to sip orangeade
from the bottle in her hands*

Suzi got up. "I've got to go," she said, and left.

The bottle of orangeade was still half full. Rick knew that Suzi loved orangeade.

Cissy decided she would have a coke. Rick's was flat, and he felt strangely uncomfortable.

As they drove up to the Ballou dooryard, Abram was at the side of the road. "What a silly donkey," Cissy said. They parked the jeep and got out.

Thomas Jefferson Tibbs appeared, rubbed against Rick's levis, then moved to inspect Cissy's trim ankles. "Go away," she said, shrilly, pushing Thomas Jefferson hard with a sandaled foot. T.J. regained his balance and dignity, and retreated, green eyes baleful.

"Where is this marvelous horse?" Cissy demanded.

"Down in his paddock, I guess," Rick said. "Come on."

The gray colt was waiting at his gate. Rick let him out, and San pushed him with his nose, inspecting him, ears pricked eagerly. Then he moved off and posed, standing straight, head high, the fine clean line of his neck blending back to the flat, sleek muscles under his steel-gray coat. Cissy looked at him. "He's cute," she said.

San turned at her voice and moved toward her, interest in his eyes, his step light, elastic, his nose out. Cissy stepped back. "Don't you slobber all over me," she warned.

"He doesn't slobber," Rick said sharply, involuntarily.

"He might," Cissy said, showing no more interest in the colt. "What do you say we go up to the lake?"

"I thought we might make a sandwich and take it up to our pond here," Rick said, looking at San.

"Some of the crowd might be at the lake," Cissy said. "Let's go there."

Rick hesitated. "OK," he said shortly. There was no one at the lake and, after a tasteless sandwich, he drove Cissy back to Woodville.

"See you tomorrow?" she said, possessively, from the sidewalk at her house.

"I'll call you," Rick said.

He turned in at the Baird Farm on the way .home. Suzi was driving the herd into the barnyard for milking. She was being very efficient and busy about it, and paid no attention to him.

"Do you want to help me with San tomorrow?" Rick asked, when a stray Jersey brought her near him.

"Can't," Suzi said bleakly.

"But you said . . ." Rick began.

"Have to work," Suzi said, closing the gate.

"Well, are you going to the dance at the Center Saturday?" Rick asked, almost shouting it as she urged the cattle up the runway into the barn.

"Don't know," Suzi said, and vanished, trim and quick in her tight levis.

Rick shook his head, got into the jeep, and cruised home. It certainly hadn't been much of a day. First Cissy and the way she'd felt about San. Now Suzi sore about something. There was no figuring girls. Horses were a lot easier.

The next day he put the saddle on San for the first time. It turned out to be a complete anticlimax. Rick showed San the saddle. He sniffed it with no particular interest. Rick put it carefully on his back. San didn't move. When Rick tightened the girth, San's ears went back a fraction of an inch, and he looked around questioningly at this confining, unfamiliar band around his belly. Then he relaxed again. The bridle, he seemed to assume, was just a halter.

But when Rick put the snaffle bit in his mouth, that was something different. He mouthed it, bounced it on his teeth, shook his head to rattle it, and worked over it with his tongue. However, he seemed to do this more as an interesting experiment than because he was bothered by the round, jointed piece of steel. Rick led him around for a few minutes. Then he took the tack off, and San immediately went back to eating grass, completely unconcerned.

The next day and the next Rick repeated the process. San continued to mouth and rattle the bit but, beyond that, accepted the whole thing as a matter of course. "Next week," Rick said to him, "I'll get on you."

Eleven

THE NEXT NIGHT WAS SATURDAY, THE NIGHT OF THE dance at the town center. There was nothing at Parnell Center except the crossroads store and the town hall. The town hall had high white pillars at the front. Its small-paned windows stretched high. Along one side were the carriage sheds from an earlier day. Inside, there was one big room with a stage. The room was used for town meetings, the grange, dances, and other special occasions.

On this particular night, when Rick drove up in his topless jeep with turned-down windshield, the big moon was just coming up over the trees, and light streamed out from the windows, casting long shadows from the groups who stood around the parking space. A harsh, staccato beat from Al Fredley and his Harmony Boys wafted over the countryside. This was the night for dress up, clean up, let go a little.

Rick parked the jeep, said hello to people clustered about, wandered up to the big front door, and took a look inside. A dance had just ended, groups were talking and laughing. There was one group of three or four

boys and one girl. Rick took it in casually, then intently.
The girl was Suzi.

Only, as he came closer, he discovered it wasn't quite
the Suzi he knew so well. This girl, slender and curved
in a yellow dress, had hair that swirled with careful
carelessness across her forehead, dropping in sleek
brown waves, the ends tightly curled, framing a piquant
face. Hidden were the freckles on the bit of a nose.
The mouth, framing those white teeth, was a discreet
but somehow tantalizing red. This was Suzi Baird? Rick
started to move in. The four boys—one a Woodville
High senior—gave no ground. Rick tried again to peer
into the laughing group. "Hi," he said.

Suzi looked at him politely, and with little interest.
"Oh, hello," she said, ever so casually.

Al Fredley and his Harmony Boys began sounding

It wasn't quite the Suzi he knew so well

off. Rick forced an opening in the phalanx of boys. "How about a dance?" he said.

Suzi's smile was bland and very gay. "After Tom and Joey and Red and Sandy here," she said, as Sandy, the senior, took her in his arms, "Oh yes, and Johnny Law outside." She whirled away.

Rick picked a slow path toward the door, through the dancing couples. Lena Baird was sitting on one of the side benches with some other women. She gave him a quizzical smile. She had her hair done, too, and looked very pretty. Rick went outside and talked with some of the crowd. He tried three times to get a dance with Suzi, cutting in, but he never did get more than a few steps.

Toward midnight he said, "Can I drive you home? I've got the jeep."

"I told Sandy I'd let him take me home," Suzi said. "We have to follow the family."

Rick drove home alone. "Good grief," he said to himself, "she didn't have to act like that just because I went around a little with Cissy Parlance."

It took a long time for him to get to sleep. The slim figure in the yellow dress kept dancing across his mind.

On Sunday Rick got on San for the first time. He asked Kink to stand by, just in case. He got on very slowly, very carefully, being extra careful not to prod San in the ribs with his toe as he mounted. Kink held the colt's bridle, but it wasn't necessary. San turned his head as Rick got on. Rick sat quietly, and he could feel the horse's heart thumping extra hard under his legs.

Rick got on San very slowly, very carefully

"It's OK, San," he said quietly, patting the colt's neck. For several minutes he sat there talking to the young horse, and then he began to feel the heartbeats slacken under him, and San's head went down. He moved a step or two, asked for his head—and began to eat grass.

In a few minutes Rick brought the colt's head up, urged him gently with his legs, and walked him out through the meadow, down a woods path and back. The colt rattled the bit, shook his head a time or two, turned one big eye back at Rick to be reassured, and did absolutely nothing else. After that it was routine.

"Confidence," Darwin Mears had said. "Get his confidence, get him to trust and rely on you, and you can do anything with him. It doesn't happen very often, this accord between a man and a horse, but when it does, it's very rewarding."

Baird Farm was like an armed camp when Rick got there at eight o'clock Monday morning. Hay is the all-important crop, and you pray for plenty of sun, a light breeze, and no rain when there is hay on the ground. The mower, with the eight-foot knife at attention, was on the big tractor. The two smaller tractors were hooked to the side delivery rake and the tedder, a machine with revolving prongs that kick the grass into the air to help dry it. The baler was ready at one side, as were two rubber-tired, flat-top wagons to bring in the bales.

"Weather man says it'll be good haying for a couple of days, anyway," Tom Baird said. "I knocked down a good piece on the south forty last night. Porky," he said to the hired man, who was dumpy, powerful and not overly bright, "you run over it with the tedder, shake it up. By the time you're half through it ought to be dry enough to start raking. Suzi, you'll run the side delivery." He swung onto the big tractor. "I'll knock down some more."

"What do you want me to do, Mr. Baird?" Rick asked. Suzi had only nodded to him, and had kept herself busy. Tom Baird hesitated.

"Can you use a hand scythe?"

"Some," Rick said.

"Well, you clean up the corners where the mower can't get. And along the ditches. After Suzi's had half an hour with the side delivery, you can start with the bull rake."

The bull rake was a huge wooden hand rake, some five feet across, the teeth a foot long, that was used to get into corners and other hard-to-reach spots. It was the low job in the hayfield.

Suzi chugged off on the small tractor. Rick walked down to the south forty. The sun was hot on his back, and he took off his shirt and swung the scythe. He was parched, his hands blistering, his face burning red when noon came and they went to the house for the workers' lunch that Lena had ready.

Suzi had agreed, briefly, that it was hot. She splashed cold water on her face at the sink. "Glad to see your freckles are back," Rick said, taking his place at the sink.

Suzi tossed her head. "They aren't back on your

friends," she said. At lunch her mother and Porky sat between him and Suzi, and he couldn't talk with her. Nobody said much anyway. The lunch was big: cold meat, baked beans, corn that Lena had put up, hot bread, apple and peach pie, and cake.

That afternoon they baled, and brought the bales to the conveyor belt, beside the barn, that carried them up to the mows. Rick didn't know how many of the fifty-pound, twine-tied, bales he hoisted from the ground to the flat tops and from the flat tops to the conveyor, but by five o'clock his back was breaking. Lena had brought them lemonade in a gallon jug, the ice clanking inside, and that had helped. But he was tired, dog-tired. Suzi looked worn out too, her face streaked with sweat and dust, her hair stringy, the back of her shirt dark with sweat.

"I'll help you get in the cows," Rick said.

She shook her head. "You're a field hand," she said. "No chores."

"I'll help you with the cows," he repeated. As she turned away to get Ulysses S. Grant, Rick took her shoulder.

"Suzi," he said, "Sunday you've got to come for the day and see San under saddle. He's wonderful."

She looked up at him for a second, her face very serious, her eyes large. "Do you really want me to?" she asked, her voice low.

"Sure I do," Rick said, "you know I do. We'll go to the pond, the three of us."

"Then I'll come," she said. She turned away quickly, so quickly that he could not see the glint of tears, bright in her eyes.

But, suddenly, he didn't feel tired at all. He felt great. They had a lot of fun rounding up the cattle from back in the trees, and he stayed on and helped with the milking. On the way home in the jeep he whistled tunelessly, joyously.

During the next month or so they put over seven thousand bales into the barn. Only one small field was rained on, and that wasn't hurt much because the grass had just been cut, and was green. Rick was a deep brown to his waist. Suzi's nose had peeled and healed and peeled again. The freckles were definitely back. So was the happy glint in her eyes.

Almost every evening, after chores, they jeeped to Rick's house, did up his animals, and then, with San leading the way, they headed for the clear, cool waters of the pond. Kink came with them sometimes, as much to watch the gray colt as anything. San frolicked in the water; he towed Rick and Suzi as they clung to his tail and to his withers; he climbed out on the bank and shook himself, drenching everyone again. And he grew and grew.

"I'll bet he's over sixteen hands," Rick said one evening before dinner when they were on the side lawn.

Suzi agreed. "Ulysses is fifteen hands, almost, and San's at least four inches taller."

The gray colt cropped grass a few feet away. Kink,

in faded chinos, blue shirt, and sneakers, drank his cider. Rick and Suzi had cokes. Suddenly, San raised his head toward them. He ambled over, put his nose out, and sniffed the cider mug beside Kink's chair.

"Hey," Kink remonstrated, "get out of that."

"What do you say we give him some," Rick said.

Kink sighed. "There goes my cider supply," he said resignedly. "All right, pour some into that white porcelain pail from the porch."

Rick got the cider. San watched with interest. Then, as Rick held the pail for him, he drank, tentatively at first, then hungrily. When the pail was empty, he rattled it, trying for the last drop. Rick beamed. "He loves the stuff. Come on, San, join the party."

San joined the party. He joined it every evening, in spite of Kink's half-hearted protests about the drain on his cider supply. When his drink was late, San rattled the white pail.

Twelve

O N SUNDAYS, AND AFTER HAYING WAS DONE ON SAT-
urday afternoons, Rick on San, and Suzi on Ulysses S. Grant, roamed the far hills and fields, exploring
deserted farms, discovering new trails, teaching the
horses to jump logs in the woods, brooks, post-and-rail
barways.

In the beginning, Rick used the saddle and bridle.
Then he gave up the saddle. It seemed a bother, and
Suzi rode bareback anyway. Then Rick gave up the
bridle and bit. It was a nuisance when San wanted to
eat grass. And, as Rick discovered around the home
farm, San responded perfectly to the pressure of a halter
on his nose, a shank against the side of his neck, and the
shifting of Rick's weight to help indicate direction.

"Well," Suzi said, "if you can ride San without a bridle, I guess I can do the same with Ulysses." So they
rode bareback with halter and rope from then on.

It was perfect, that summer, Rick thought. Perfect,
except for one thing. Before long he would have to make
a decision, *the* decision. He talked it over, finally, with
Suzi, as the two horses ambled side by side down a
country lane one afternoon late in August.

"Mr. Corcoran says it's my duty to put San on the track, to race him. Mr. Mears says it's my decision. What do you think?"

Suzi did not answer him for a minute. The horses plodded down the mossy lane, San's footsteps light and quick, Ulysses' sturdy and steady.

"I don't know, Rick," she said, at last, "I—I just don't believe in borrowing trouble. You don't have to decide until next spring. Maybe something will happen then, or before then, to help you make up your mind. Won't that be time enough?"

She was right, as it turned out. Something did happen to show him. Two things happened.

On the first day of school, early in September, Rick and Suzi rode on the bus together. She had on a blue dress with a narrow white band at her throat and wrists. "Nervous?" he asked. She smiled quickly, nodding. "A little," she confessed. "It's just the first day," she said, "and that long walk up the sidewalk from where the bus drops us. What do they call it—Inspection Walk?"

Rick shrugged. "Just a bunch of upper-class girls and a few guys, looking over the new faces," he said, "nothing to worry about."

Mr. Dotham, principal of the Woodville Union High School, bald, harassed, shiny-suited, was at an upper window as they got off the bus and began the seventy-five-yard walk to the high-pillared portico, thronged with older girls and boys. Suddenly the principal grunted.

"What's the matter?" one of his teachers asked.

"Nothing," Dotham said. "It's just that you hear all this talk about the teen-agers, how hard-shelled they are, how thoughtless, and then you see a little thing like this, and it makes you wonder."

"What?" the teacher pursued.

"Young Ballou—you know, head of student government, big man in his class—walking up Inspection with some little freshman, obviously scared. So, he takes her hand, just for a second. Tells her he's with her, tells that bunch of hawks to leave her alone. Sort of a nice thing. Well, let's get going. Another year's begun."

During the winter Rick read everything he could find about horse-racing. A book about famous horses fascinated him.

"Gee, Kink," he said, "the money they make. Over a million dollars, some of them. They fly all over the world in special planes, have their own railroad cars and vans, their own exercise boys and blacksmiths and all, take their own water with them. Boy, what you could do with the money they take in."

"Only a very few of them ever do that," Kink reminded him drily.

"Oh sure," Rick admitted, getting up to throw another log on the fire, "but there isn't one of them as well put together as San. What a sight that would be—San under a blanket of roses. Some glamour."

Kink gave him a long, quizzical look. Then he went back to his book.

One morning in May when the sun was especially bright, the beginning of summer warmth in its rays, San was at the distant side of the great, sweeping meadow that lay behind the barn. He and Abram had been nosing about, looking for tender shoots. Abram started back to the barn, walking intently, steps short and choppy. He had covered a hundred yards, when San realized, suddenly, that he was left alone. He whinnied once, piercingly, protestingly, and then, with one great thrust of his hind quarters, he became vibrantly alive, wild-eyed, and in full stride.

Never had Rick seen a horse run with the floating ease, the lightness, the quickness, the compact drive that

He became vibrantly alive, wild-eyed, in full stride

San showed as he flew over the meadow. Abram pulled aside in fright, like a pedestrian on a throughway, as the gray colt roared by him and into the barnyard. Albert fled with frantic squawks, herding his hens under a bush. Thomas Jefferson Tibbs jumped, ears tight back, up the nearest tree. Tenderloin bellowed. Rose of Washington Square looked up in matronly amazement. And San propped to a dead halt, legs stiff, dirt flying, and stood there, head high, nostrils flaring, veins standing out across his coat, all the great strength of him keyed to the highest pitch.

"Man, oh man," Rick whispered to himself, "he's the fastest thing I've ever seen. He flies." His mind was made up then, in that minute. San must have his chance.

Late that afternoon Rick jeeped over to Bellemead with Kink. "You sure you want to do this?" Kink said dubiously, and Rick nodded.

"I have to," he said, "I'd never feel right unless I did it. I'd always wonder just how good he might have been."

Darwin Mears was in his cottage. "All right," he said, and there was a gleam in his eye. He was, after all, a racing man. "You've decided. Now the thing is to figure out how to get it done best."

He considered things for a minute or more. "I've thought about this some," he said, "in case you did decide. I'd like to handle the horse myself, but it never would do. Too close to home"—with a glance toward the big house—"too many complications. What we want is a top man, but one who's not involved hereabouts. I think

Abe Marvin is our man. He knows his business, he's reliable, and he's at a track not too far away."

"You mean," Kink said, "that he trains for several people, not just one stable?"

Mears nodded. "That's right," he said, "he's an independent. And a pretty dour, sour character. Very fussy about what he handles, and who for. He can afford to be. But"—and he smiled slightly—"I think he'd take this colt, if I were to ask him. Do you want to go over with me and talk to Abe?"

Kink looked at Rick. The boy nodded, only half hesitating. "This will cost something," Darwin Mears warned. "Likely five hundred a month, plus."

"I guess we can handle it," Kink said soberly. "I signed up two top assignments last month."

Darwin Mears had one more warning. "Don't get your hopes up," he said to Rick. "Just because a horse can fly over a meadow, doesn't mean, necessarily, he'll be a race horse. There's more to it than that, a lot more. You still want to go?" Rick nodded again.

Two days later they went to see Abe Marvin. Rick had never been to a big track, and he stared, fascinated, as Kink drove them past the huge grandstand, deserted now at mid-morning, along the track, freshly harrowed, and into the stable area. The stables were long, low rows of box stalls, the roof brought out ten feet or so beyond the front of the stalls to give protection and to make a covered area for working on a horse.

Exercise boys lolled in the sun. Their work was done

in the early morning. Grooms, known as "swipes," cleaned (or "cuffed off" as it was called) Thoroughbreds that were cross-tied with a shank, or cotton rope, running from each side of the animal's halter to keep him standing steady in the runway. Saddles crowded the racks. Leg bandages dried from lines. Horses were led about slowly. It was another world to Rick—the people different, quiet moving, soft-spoken, very sure, very confident. The smells were different: liniment, a hoof smoking as the blacksmith shod hot, neatsfoot oil, leather, hay, and horses. Horses were everywhere—beautiful hard-muscled horses. And over it all, a tension, a feeling of getting ready, of preparation for something big.

Abe Marvin was in front of Barn Three, watching one of his horses being fitted to racing plates. He was squat, thick-set, heavy-shouldered. His white shirt was open at the throat, and he wore a felt hat far back on his head. He showed a fleeting brightness and cordiality at the sight of Darwin Mears, and then lapsed into taciturnity, listening without expression as Darwin Mears sketched the story of the colt from its birth to now.

When Mears had finished there was silence. Abe Marvin stared out over the track. Rick watched him, hypnotized. After a while, Marvin spoke. "I take it this colt has been a pet."

Rick remembered, suddenly, Darwin Mears' definition of the usual concept of a pet—a lap-dog type, a spoiled animal. "I take good care of him," he said, his voice strangely sharp, "but he does what I want him to when I ask him."

Abe Marvin said to Rick: "To me, horses are a business"

Abe Marvin looked at him, as if seeing him for the first time. "You and I," he said, "likely look at this thing different. To me, horses are a business. I like them, sure, or I wouldn't be here, but there's no sentiment. If I took this colt it would be two months, maybe three, before he was ready. And," he said, looking squarely at Rick, "he'd be in my hands. Just mine. You don't see him at all. Ever. At least, not till I say so. No phone calls or interfering. When I get a spot for him, or have something to report, I'll let you know. You can sit in the stands and watch him run. On those terms I might do it—because Darwin here is an old friend."

Abe Marvin became interested in something else.

He moved over to the blacksmith. Darwin Mears looked at Rick. Rick looked at Kink.

"Are you sure you want to go ahead with this?" Kink asked.

Rick tried not to think, tried only to say the words he thought he must say, the hardest words he had ever tried to speak. "I—I guess, yes," he said, "I do."

Darwin Mears spoke quickly. "All right," he said, "I'll make the arrangements." He talked at some length to the trainer, who then went back to his work without even looking at the Ballous again.

It was a long ride home. "What will they do with him?" Rick asked after a heavy silence. He was alone in the back seat, and Darwin Mears turned slightly to talk to him.

"They'll gallop him every morning, early," he said, "to strengthen his wind, muscle him up, give him the feel of the track and of running with other horses. They'll teach him about the starting gate and to make a quick getaway, to run on the bit, to respond quickly to the jockey. And various other things that go to make a race horse." He talked on and on about horses he had trained, races he had won and lost, and Rick sank back on the seat and tried not to think about the fears that were trying to crowd all else out of his mind.

When they were close to Bellemead, Darwin Mears said, "I'll send the trailer for him, first thing in the morning," as if he were afraid they might change their minds.

The gray colt whinnied from his paddock when he heard father and son returning. Kink took Rick's shoulder. "Don't make it too hard for yourself, son," he said, and Rick managed a nod.

He did pretty well through the long night. In the morning the trailer rattled up the drive. Darwin Mears and one of the Bellemead hands tried to load the colt. At the backdrop he stopped, pulling away. They made three attempts to get him into the trailer, and he balked each time.

"Give me the shank," Rick said. He did not look back at San, but merely walked into the narrow trailer stall, and the big colt followed him unhesitatingly, trustingly.

They buckled the leather-covered chain behind the horse, and put up the heavy backdrop. The colt whinnied once as the trailer rumbled down the drive, and Rick turned and walked to the haven of the barn, running the last few steps.

After a while, a long while, he went out and through the meadows, into the woods, walking all day, anywhere, everywhere, stumbling sometimes because he could not see. Long after dark he came back to the house and to his room.

Thirteen

EVEN THE ANIMALS ON THE FARM WERE DIFFERENT, Rick thought, in the first days that followed. They seemed subdued, as if they missed something. Suzi was good for him.

"I know how you feel," she said on the bus, her hand light on his arm, "but you've made up your mind and you have to see it through."

Darwin Mears was matter-of-fact when Rick jeeped over to see him a week later. "Haven't heard a word," he said, "which is good news. When they have trouble they call you." He looked sharply at Rick. "Don't be so gloomy, son," he said, "your colt is all right. Horses adjust very quickly, never forget that. Why," he said, jokingly, "he's probably forgotten all about you by now."

"He'll never forget me," Rick said.

When high school was over for the summer, Rick went to work for Tom Baird again. He liked farming. The feeling of producing something—milk, hay, corn, timber—was satisfying, tangible.

"It's hard work," Suzi said, when he tried to tell her how he felt, "and not much money. But I love it, too."

116

The work in the fields left him tired and he could, finally, sleep at night. He wished now that he had never built the stall beside his bedroom, but it was there, and he had to accept it. Later it might be taken down.

Slade Corcoran dropped in after three weeks, all smiles, very affable, very friendly. They sat on the terrace in the warm Sunday morning sunshine.

"The colt is doing fine," Corcoran said, lighting a thick cigar. "I haven't seen him—very touchy man, that Marvin—but I have friends, contacts, at the track. They had a few problems at first. Apparently he wasn't interested in running any distance, but they straightened that out. Very impressive looking colt, they say, in excellent condition. You did a good job, Rick." He spoke as if Rick's part were finished.

"Of course," he went on, smiling, "we didn't do such a bad job ourselves, breeding him. He could be a credit to Bellemead Stud."

"I'll let you know," he said, as he was leaving, gunning the motor in the Jaguar, "when I get more information." He waved as the car rumbled down the hill.

Rick frowned. "He acts as if he owned San," he said.

Kink shrugged. "Don't worry about it," he said, shuffling the Sunday paper, "the colt's registered in your name. It's just Slade's way." Rick grumbled, but it was the only contact he'd had with San, and better than nothing. Ten days later Corcoran came by again.

"Apparently," he said, leaning against his car, "your colt has Abe Marvin puzzled. They say he has tremendous stride, great power, really phenomenal, but he

117

doesn't always try. Doesn't put out, isn't a competitor."

"He's never competed," Rick said drily, almost bitterly.

"Maybe that's it," Corcoran agreed. "Maybe when he goes racing it will put the fire into him. Hope so."

"Any idea when Marvin might find a spot for him?" Kink asked.

Slade Corcoran shook his head. "I haven't heard," he admitted, "but I'll keep in touch."

Slade Corcoran wasn't the first to let them know.

It was five weeks later, almost the end of July, when the phone rang one evening.

"I've got a spot for your Sans Peur colt," Abe Marvin said, "third race, Saturday, August fourth. It's a five-thousand-dollar added purse, three years and up." Rick gasped.

"But," Marvin went on, "I'm going to ask you not to even come down and see him when we're saddling in the paddock. I don't want him upset."

"How—how is he doing?" Rick asked.

"He *could*," Abe Marvin said, after a second's silence. "I'll see you after the race Saturday." The phone clicked dead. Rick hung up slowly.

"I heard some of it," Kink said. "Fill me in." Rick did.

"Well," Kink said, reassuringly, "at least we'll know. There'll be no more waiting."

The news got around fast. Slade Corcoran came up the next morning. "Our colt is running August fourth . . ." he began.

"We knew," Kink told him, calmly, "our trainer called."

Corcoran wasn't bothered. "Well," he said, puffing slightly, "I've got a box at the track. Used to be on the commission, you know. Keep up my connections. And I'd like to have you as my guests that day. Age just might be a factor, you know, minors sometimes not allowed and all, but I can bring anyone I want. Glad to have you."

"Thank you, sir," Rick said, meaning it, "but, that is, would it be all right, I mean might I bring Suzi Baird with me?"

Slade Corcoran could be very pleasant. "Why not," he said, expansively, "make it Parnell Center Day. Hope we'll have something to celebrate. I'll be in touch."

By ten o'clock on Saturday, August fourth, it was already hot, promising to be scorching later. Rick was fidgeting to go.

"There's no rush," Kink said, trying to calm him, "Corcoran said to be at Bellemead by eleven. We'll go in one of his cars."

They picked up Suzi a bit before eleven. She had on the blue dress, the one that Rick liked, with the narrow band of white at the throat and cuffs. "It'll bring us luck," he said.

Slade Corcoran was in no hurry. "It's only a two hours' drive," he said. "We'll have a bite of lunch in the clubhouse. Probably sit right there."

Darwin Mears was in front with Corcoran in the big black sedan. No one said much. After a while Suzi's hand found Rick's, and they rode most of the way in silence.

The parking spaces at the track stretched for acres,

119

their asphalt paving shimmering in the heat. Cars were piling in. Slade Corcoran drove to the clubhouse entrance and turned the car over to an attendant. "This way," he said, shepherding them through the gate.

"Good afternoon, Mr. Corcoran." "Fine day, Mr. Corcoran." "Nice to see you again, Mr. Corcoran," came from all sides.

Pennants waved gaily above the grandstand. The shirt-sleeved crowd ebbed and flowed. Fans, in the lower seats, pored over dope sheets. The hum and murmur of the crowd were gathering slowly to a roar. Hawkers yelled, offering their tip sheets and programs.

Rick watched it all from the table in the clubhouse above. It was cooler up there, but still very hot. The tablecloths were heavy white, the waiters murmured politely, moved soft-footed. Ice clinked in glasses.

"Just a sandwich," Rick said. His mouth and throat were dry, his hands hot and damp. Down there, somewhere, was his colt, Sans Peur. Down there on the track in front of him Sans Peur would come out, after a while, and run his race. He tried the sandwich and it was dry and tasteless. "No thanks," he said, "nothing more."

Suzi sat beside him, calling his attention to things below, trying to keep him occupied. Slade Corcoran moved off to chat with friends. Darwin Mears studied the record sheets. At two o'clock they ran the first race, and Rick watched the horses come out from the paddock, through the narrow runway, the jockeys gay in their colors, perched in the tiny saddles like monkeys.

The Thoroughbreds were lean, trim, stepping dain-

120

tily, heads high. Some wore blinkers. Some had lead ponies, outriders, to bring them in, to calm them. They moved down the track to the towering, spider-like starting gate. They maneuvered behind it. They were led in. He watched the race with no interest. There would be one more. And then there would be his race.

Slade Corcoran came back to the table while the second race was being run. "If you move over to the far end here," he said, "and use these field glasses, you just might catch a glimpse of your horse being saddled in the paddock."

Rick went over with Suzi, but they couldn't see much. "I think I saw his head," Suzi said, after Rick had given up. The paddock was off at too great an angle. All you could see were hatless men, and cigars, and people whispering behind their hands. The boy and girl went back to the table.

The track was freshly harrowed now, and the furrow lines ran, dwindling, out of sight at the first turn. It made you dizzy, almost, looking at them. The judges' and stewards' stand was almost directly across the track from their table in the clubhouse. Rick watched the men there, talking, gesticulating.

The infield was a close-trimmed green and there was a lake with swans and ducks, with a man-made island or two in the sparkling water. The heat shimmered up, making glassy waves across the infield. The gay pennants fluttered and died as the breeze gave up. Rick looked at his program again. It was creased and damp in his hot hands.

121

"Number 5," it said, "gray colt Sans Peur, by *Mon Oncle—Never Fear. Owner R. Ballou. Jockey C. Melville." Who was C. Melville? He had never heard of him.

The odds on the tote board flickered and changed. Slade Corcoran grunted and got up. "Thirty to one," he said, "too good to miss." He looked at Darwin Mears, who nodded. He looked at Kink. Kink shook his head. Slade Corcoran called a boy to run his errand. The bugle blew to post.

The line of horses appeared slowly in the narrow runway. Rick felt his throat go tight, constricting tight. He got up and moved to the front so that he could see better. Suzi was with him, and her hand found his again.

"It's going to be all right, Rick," she said, "everything is going to be all right." He nodded, or tried to, and then he saw the gray colt come through the end of the runway, and a band seemed to tighten hard across his chest.

Sans Peur walked slowly, with his head up, and he looked quietly at the people lining the runway. The groom leading him kept a tight rein and Sans Peur paid him no attention. He walked as if this were a routine duty, that he knew he must do it, and that he would. His eyes were bright, alert, and his coat gleamed. He was hard, flat-muscled, and ready, but there was a change, a difference.

"It's gone," Kink thought, "that wonderful curiosity, that eagerness, that certainty that he's among friends. He's automatic now. But he sure is beautiful."

People around were saying "Look at that gray. Fine put-together thing. Can he run? No record."

122

The crowd murmured and hummed below them, and Rick stood there, staring down, watching the gray colt as it moved off, his hands slowly shredding the program that was damp and wadded now.

The horses turned above the starting gate, working back into it, and he saw the gray colt move calmly into the Number 5 slot. For this race the gate was at the far end of the track: the horses would pass in front of the grandstand twice.

There was, suddenly, a quick hush over the stands, and then there was the cry, "They're off!" The gates burst open and they shot out, moving for position, in front of the clubhouse, almost, before he could place the gray horse.

At last he saw him, just a bit on the outside, with running room, and then the gray colt, Sans Peur, ran. He ran the way you have seldom seen a horse run, with great distance-eating strides, low and flying and easy, his hoofs hardly touching the ground, and the great and beautiful rhythm of him. So that people rose and yelled with the surge of admiration and wonder and frenzy almost, with, somehow, the feeling that history was being made in front of them.

At the turn into the back stretch the gray colt was twenty lengths, at least twenty lengths, ahead of the struggling field, and the roar and swell of the crowd below and around Rick was stifling, the heat forgotten.

He stood there, the white-clothed table behind him, looking out at the gray colt—his colt—and the thought came and choked him, and he sobbed involuntarily, just

The gray was forty lengths in front of the pack

once. "All right," he thought, "I've lost him. I've lost that friend who loved the woods and the fields with me. I've lost him to crowds and yells and planes and vans and trains and money, and it's a thing I've had to do because he can run this way, because this is his life."

There was no crowd around him now, no Slade Corcoran pounding on the table, no Suzi, no Kink. There was just the gray horse out there across the track, and he watched him dumbly, silently, saying goodby.

They came around the clubhouse turn now, and the gray was forty lengths in front of the pack, floating with that great effortless stride, the jockey a nothing on his back, a passenger. And then, with only two hundred yards or less to the finish line, he slowed.

He slowed, veering out for room, and then, without hesitation, he took three strides, jumped the infield fence and, in a leisurely, calculated gallop, ears up in anticipation, he headed for the sparkling pond, jumping far out into the cool, blue waters, his jockey flying free, the ducks and swans fleeing in squawking horror.

No one who was at the track that day will ever forget, probably, the scene that followed—the officials running, the jockey wading out dripping, whip in hand, the gray colt up to his belly and then rolling in the cool, cool waters.

Corcoran was paralyzed, but Kink seemed to know what to do. "Come on," he said, and they were down the stairs and out of the small gate and across the track into the infield, with someone shouting "You can't . . ." as Rick went through with Suzi clutching his hand, feet flying.

They were into the infield and out to the pond, and Rick said, his voice authoritative, commanding, "Let me through there. It's my colt."

People drew back for a second, looking at him, and he took over. "San," he called, "come on, San. Out of there. Time to come out." He called it two, three times, and then the gray colt turned his head, questioningly, the shallow water up to his belly.

Then he moved, pushing his way out, majestically, dripping, and Rick was beside him, taking the reins, and they moved back toward the stable area, following Abe Marvin, the hum and roar and buzz of the crowd like a curtain behind them.

"All right," Abe Marvin said "scram. Out of here," to the deep circle of hangers on, grooms, swipes, exercise boys, reporters, and cameramen around the stall at Barn Three. Reluctantly, they moved away.

"I've had a lot of things happen to me in this game," Abe Marvin said, as they stripped the saddle and the dripping pad from the gray colt, "but never this."

Rick stood at the gray's head, and Abe Marvin went on. "Of course, it doesn't amount to much. We can straighten him out of a thing like this easy enough. This colt," he said, with a new respect in his voice, "is apt to make you a lot of money, son."

Rick scarcely heard him, his hand moving automatically in the spot on San's shoulder that he liked to have scratched. Slade Corcoran was with Kink at one side, talking vigorously. Kink beckoned Rick over.

Rick was beside him, taking the reins,

"Mr. Corcoran," he said to Rick, very calm despite the noise and dust and confusion beyond, "has something he wants to say to you."

Rick looked at the fat, sweating man. Slade Corcoran's face was red, his eyes bright and eager, little flecks of foam at the corners of his mouth. "I told your father," he said, "you being under age, that I was prepared to offer you a handsome price for this colt. He's still untried, really, but I'd give you . . ." He named a sum, and Rick heard Suzi gasp behind him. It was a fortune. Kink watched him carefully, that questioning smile on his lips.

It was, Rick thought, a simple thing, it was such a very simple thing. He heard his father say, "It's up to you, son." Then Rick laughed. It was a joyful, clear laugh and he felt better than he ever had.

and they moved toward the stable area

"Thank you, sir," he said, "but I guess San showed me something this afternoon. I guess he told me. I think we'll go on home. All of us." He turned to Darwin Mears. "Could you have a van pick him up this afternoon? You know these truckers." Darwin Mears nodded.

It was eight o'clock that evening, with the red hot ball of sun going slowly down on the horizon. Richard Jonathan (Rick) Ballou leaned on the far pasture fence. Suzi Baird, her blue dress miraculously still trim and neat, leaned beside him, one slender ankle perched above the bottom rail. Abram grazed. Thomas Jefferson Tibbs sharpened his claws on a fence post. Tenderloin grunted amiably in his paddock. Rose of Washington Square peered in near-sighted interest. And the gray colt, Sans Peur, by *Mon Oncle out of Never Fear, cropped grass in front of them all with an easy, relaxed manner.

"You know," Rick said, "when we get our farm, we just might raise some Thoroughbreds. Maybe we'll make hunters of them."

Suzi Baird nodded. "Yes," she said, matter-of-factly, "I think that would be fun. Particularly if they turned out like San."

The colt raised his head and looked at them in complete contentment, as if he had known all along that he would be back home—for keeps.